This book should be returned to any branch of the
Lancashire County Library on or before the date shown

Lancashire County Library
Bowran Street
Preston PR1 2UX

Lancashire
County Council

www.lancashire.gov.uk/libraries

LL1(A)

D0452297

Free pet pigs for all (you are not allowed to eat them though!)
—FREDDIE, age 9

Children to choose their own name, but until they can talk, they are all called Bert!
—GABI, age 11

Blindfold robbers so they can't see who to rob.
—FRASER, age 8 and CAMERON, age 5

WHAT WOULD YOU DO?

Cows get people farms.
—FREDDIE, age 9

Invent a 99p coin. It would make paying for stuff much easier.
—JOE, age 12

Sheep get sheep villages.
—FREDDIE, age 9

All children get to vote
which teacher they want.
—GABI, age 11

On Mondays, at
2:35 pm, there is
a jelly fight.
—FREDDIE, age 9

Everyone MUST
feed ducks
every Tuesday.
—FREDDIE, age 9

Children need only
shower/bath on Sundays.
—GABI, age 11

Put up signs saying
'Welcome to France'
at borders to confuse
people when they arrive.
—FRASER, age 8 and CAMERON, age 5

Develop a chip that
children can put in
their ears to download
all knowledge they need.
—GABI, age 11

THE VOTE  JOE MANIFESTO

- ARE YOU FED UP OF LIVING IN A COUNTRY LED BY GREEDY BUMBLING WARTHOGS?*

- THEN LOOK NO FURTHER THAN JOE PERKINS!

- JOE SPOKE UP FOR A SOCIETY IN NEED OF CHANGE, HIS VIEWS WENT VIRAL AND TODAY YOU CAN REAP THE BENEFITS OF HIS YOUTHFUL WISDOM BY VOTING . . . !

- YES TO CATS IN HATS!

- YES TO BANANA SHAPED BUSES!

- YES TO FANCY DRESS FRIDAYS (BUT ON A THURSDAY)!

- YES TO JOE PERKINS FOR PRIME MINISTER!!

*OTHERWISE KNOWN AS GROWN-UPS

For my boys Joe and Harry
Love, always

OXFORD
UNIVERSITY PRESS

Great Clarendon Street, Oxford OX2 6DP
Oxford University Press is a department of the University of Oxford.
It furthers the University's objective of excellence in research, scholarship,
and education by publishing worldwide

Oxford is a registered trade mark of Oxford University Press
in the UK and in certain other countries

Text and illustration © Tom McLaughlin 2015
The moral rights of the author and illustrator have been asserted

Database right Oxford University Press (maker)

First published 2015

British Library Cataloguing in Publication Data

Data available

ISBN: 978-0-19-273774-8

3 5 7 9 10 8 6 4 2

Printed in Great Britain
Paper used in the production of this book is a natural,
recyclable product made from wood grown in sustainable forests
The manufacturing process conforms to the environmental
regulations of the country of origin.

THE Accidental...
PRIME MINISTER

Written and
illustrated by
Tom
McLaughlin

OXFORD
UNIVERSITY PRESS

I DON'T LIKE MONDAYS

'**B**LEEEEEEEEEEEP!'

There are many awful sounds in this world. Fingernails down the blackboard, Mum singing the theme tune to Match of the Day in the shower, bagpipes being played badly, in fact bagpipes being played brilliantly as well. But there are none worse than the sound of an alarm clock early on a Monday.

'Why are mornings so early?' Joe muttered to himself, before trying to grab his alarm clock, missing it and falling out of bed. This was not uncommon for Joe.

He often fell, even when no falling was required. He was one of life's great fallers. He fell into rooms, he fell out of them again. He even managed the almost impossible task of falling upstairs which, let me tell you, is no mean feat. Joe's life was a constant battle with gravity, one in which gravity clearly had the upper hand. He picked himself up from the bedroom floor and set about trying to get dressed without opening his eyes. It was a trick that he tried to help fool his sleepy head that he was still in bed. The downside was it made putting pants on very tricky indeed. Up to that point, putting on underwear with his eyes shut was as close to living on the edge as Joe's life got.

Joe lived in a tiny house in London with his mum. Dad had disappeared before Joe was born and he didn't have any brothers or sisters. The nearest he ever came to having a sibling was the time when a cat from down the street came to stay for ten days last year. Other than Mr Tiddles, it had only ever been the two of them. Joe's mum was a park warden, and that meant she spent most of her days making sure that the flowers were looked after and no dogs were doing their doings where they shouldn't.

It was a job she loved, and Joe loved her working there too. Joe's house didn't have a garden, just a tiny yard, the sort of place where you'd graze your knee if you fell over. Which as you know, is something Joe did a lot. So the park always felt like his and Mum's garden. When Mum wasn't in the park, pruning flowers and shouting at dog owners, she was in the kitchen cooking. It was her thing. She would stop off at the shops and buy the bags of food that no one else wanted, which she'd use for inspiration in the kitchen, thinking up extraordinarily weird recipes with which to torture . . . I mean impress, Joe. Joe knew that it was really because money was sometimes tight, but it meant that meal times were never dull—I mean, who can forget the cheese salad with onion gravy, or the plum tandoori crumble? Apart from the odd, odd meal, Joe's life was pretty unremarkable. Apart from . . .

BRRRRIIIIIIIIING!

Just then the doorbell rang.

'LET ME IN, IT'S AN EMERGENCY!' came the exasperated cry from the other side.

Joe's mum opened the door and there stood Ajay, Joe's oldest and best friend.

'What is it, Ajay?' Joe's mum said, sounding panic-stricken.

'I smell your world-famous fresh tea and toast with sour rhubarb jam, Mrs P, and I need a fix!' Ajay grinned and waggled an eyebrow up and down. Ajay was the only person in the world who found Joe's mum's cooking not only edible, but enjoyable too. Then again, Ajay did once eat a fingerful of his own earwax in Geography for a bet, so it's fair to say he probably hasn't got the most sophisticated palate.

'Oh, Ajay, doesn't your mother feed you?' Joe's mum asked, rolling her eyes. But she was well used to Ajay's tardis-like stomach.

'Breakfast is the most important meal of the day, Mrs P, that's why I make it my business to have as many as possible. Got any pork pies?' Ajay grinned, pushing past her in the direction of the breakfast table.

'You know I hate those things, Ajay!' Mum said, shaking her head. 'I think it's the jelly—it makes me squeamish.'

Ajay and Joe had been friends since they were at nursery when they found out they had the same birthday. And let me tell you, when you're three, that sort of thing blows your mind, which pretty much means you're destined to be bestest friends for life. If it wasn't for Ajay, school would be nothing more than a yawn factory. Ajay was the sort of boy who made even the dullest, dreariest things in life seem a giggle. He was always scheming, always thinking of a plan to make the teacher laugh. Or trying to figure out how they were both going to become millionaires by next Tuesday. These plans nearly always involved Joe and nearly always failed—but that was half the fun.

Ajay was just about to tuck into his tea and toast dripping in sour rhubarb jam when there was a loud clatter from the letterbox as an important-looking brown envelope landed on the mat.

'Bit early for the post isn't it?' Mum said. 'Ooh, it says Special Delivery.' She opened it, and unfolded the letter.

Joe knew instantly that something was wrong. He could see it on Mum's face.

'What is it, Mum?' Joe asked.

'Yeah, Mrs P, what's happened?' Ajay asked too.

'It's the park . . . they've shut it down.'

For a second no one said a word. Joe and Ajay looked at each other, then back at Joe's mum. Her face was pale, her jaw dropped open. She stared at the letter, her eyes watery and ready to spill over with tears.

'Shut the park!' Joe said furiously. 'They can't do that, it's . . . it's the park!'

'Yeah, everyone loves that place!' Ajay joined in.

'You boys best get to school, or you'll be late,' said Mum, her voice all shaky.

'But what about . . . ?' Joe started to say.

'You leave that to me, I don't want you worrying.' Mum tried to smile, but it didn't reach her eyes. If she was trying to reassure Joe, it wasn't working. He knew his mum needed that job—how else was she supposed to put sweet-and-sour spaghetti on the table?

'Don't worry, Mum, I'll . . . I'll think of something.'

Joe's mum just nodded, turning away to wipe her eyes.

Joe and Ajay grabbed their bags and reluctantly headed out of the door. Neither of them said anything for what seemed like ages.

'You all right, man?' Ajay asked, breaking the silence.

'I don't know . . . I can't believe they've closed the park. I mean, why?!' Joe said in disbelief.

'Dunno,' Ajay shrugged. 'But I know a man who might,' he said, pointing down the road.

As they turned the corner at the top of Joe's street they saw a man in the distance. He had a ladder and toolbox and was busy hammering a sign into the park gates. This made Joe's blood boil. If Mum had been there she would have given him what for—no one hammers anything into anything without her say-so first.

'Oi!' Ajay yelled, 'what are you doing?'

Joe read the sign: 'Under development.'

'What's going on?' Joe asked. 'Why have you closed the park?'

The man stopped what he was doing and shrugged. 'They don't tell me anything—I'm just the bloke who hammers things.'

Joe read the rest of the sign.

UNDER DEVELOPMENT

'THIS NOTICE HEREBY DECLARES THAT ST GEORGE'S PARK IS CLOSED WITH IMMEDIATE EFFECT AND THAT FROM 1ST OF JULY, THIS PARK WILL BE REDEVELOPED AND A NEW BLOCK OF LUXURY FLATS WILL BE BUILT—DEPARTMENT OF PROGRESS'

Underneath the notice was a drawing of a posh building, tall and made of glass. It had pictures of smiling people chatting and drinking coffee outside. Joe and Ajay looked through the park gates and could already see diggers moving in, ready to tear the playground apart.

'This can't be happening,' Joe muttered, blinking back the tears. This was the place where he and Ajay hung out. Where they used to plot how they were going to become mega rich, and plan what to do if the world got taken over by zombies. This was the place where Joe and Ajay used to play football—or rather where Ajay would kick the ball and Joe would try to get out of the way of it before it hit him in the face. And now it was going to be turned into flats! Why wasn't anyone stopping this?

''Ello 'ello, anything I can do?'

Joe turned to see a policeman, standing by the sign and looking down at Joe and Ajay.

'Yes!' Joe gasped. 'Stop this man from closing the park!'

'Yes officer,' Ajay joined in, 'arrest this man.'

'Eh?' said the man hammering. 'What did *I* do?'

'You're closing the park!' Ajay yelled at him.

'I told you, I'm just the bloke who does the hammering, I'm not closing anything.'

Just then, a group of police motorcycle outriders whizzed past, sirens screaming and lights flashing as they went. It was like something from a movie, only it was happening in their street.

'What on earth!' the man on the ladder said, nearly but, rather disappointingly, not falling off.

'Ooooh!' said Ajay, glaring wide-eyed at the convoy of flashing blue lights and sirens. 'Do you think there's been a bank robbery? Or maybe aliens have landed!'

'Oh, I hope it's an alien invasion!' said Joe. 'We'd definitely get the day off school for that.'

'It's the Prime Minister,' said the policeman. 'He's visiting here today and I'm here as back-up.'

'You mean you're not here to stop them closing the park?' Joe said.

'Oh no, looks like the park's had it,' he said, peering at the sign. 'Shame, I used to play here as a kid.'

'Where is the Prime Minister visiting?' Joe asked.

'A school I think . . . Yes, it's definitely a school.'

There was only one school down that end of the road. Joe and Ajay's school. Ajay and Joe looked at each other and, without saying a word, they grabbed their bags and ran. Well, Ajay ran, Joe tripped over his laces.

'I bet he can save the park!' Joe yelled, picking himself up.

'Bound to!' Ajay grinned. 'At the very least we'll probably get out of double Algebra!'

'This is even better than the time that dog came in the playground and pooed on the netball court!' yelled Joe.

'Well, I don't know, that was a pretty special day,' said Ajay seriously, 'but it's definitely up there.'

By the time Ajay and Joe got to school there was a huge crowd already there, of excited schoolchildren, policemen, TV reporters, and cross-looking members of the public. There, at the front of the crowd, stood the headmaster, Mr Brooks.

Ajay nudged Joe. 'Mr Brooks looks . . . well, really weird. Has he combed his hair differently?'

Mr Brooks had indeed combed his hair, but that wasn't it. Suddenly Joe figured it out.

'I know, I know! He's smiling!'

'Oh yeah,' Ajay realized. 'It's really creepy, isn't it?'

'What's going on, Mr Brooks?' said Joe.

Mr Brooks sighed impatiently. 'Oh no, not you two! I warn you—any mischief and you'll be for the high jump!'

'Is the Prime Minister coming, sir?' Ajay asked, looking at the big black limo that had just pulled up behind the police motorcycles.

'Yes. It was supposed to be a secret, you know, for security reasons, seeing as how he's pretty much hated by most people these days. But some buffoon must have told the papers. I mean, look at all these cameras!' he said, suddenly grinning and running a licked finger over one eyebrow.

The doors of the black limo opened and out stepped a stout man in a mud-coloured suit. He had a red, wobbly face, in the middle of which sat a bulbous nose, like a cherry on a particularly disgusting trifle. The man dabbed his sweaty face with a hanky and attempted to flatten his wispy hair with a clammy hand.

The man in question was Percival T. Duckholm. He was the Prime Minister of Great Britain and, it's fair to say, one of the most disliked men in the land. He was the kind of man who would not only sell his grandmother for a quick buck, but he'd also try to sell your grandmother too. In fact, if you've got a moment I suggest you give her a quick ring and tell her not to answer the door to any trifle-faced Prime Ministers. Percival T. Duckholm was also one of the rudest men you're ever likely to meet. He liked to shout at people—in fact, shouting was his most favourite thing in the world. He'd shout in the morning at breakfast to his poor wife and pale children. Then he'd have a bath and shout a bit in there.

Then he'd get dressed and shout about how he couldn't find his socks, then he'd go to work and shouty-shout-shout until lunch, before it all got too much and he had to have a nap until it was home time.

You may well say, surely he can't be this bad? Surely someone must like him—I mean, he did manage to become Prime Minister after all? Well, the simple truth is the man he was up against was even more loathsome. I know, it's hard to believe. But let me tell you about Melvyn Thwick, a man so obnoxious that if you ever got to meet him it would take all your strength not to vomit through your nose just to be in the same room as him. He had greasy hair, terrible breath and dandruff so bad, you'd think winter had come early by looking at the state of his shoulders. He picked his nose with all the eagerness and desperation of a man looking for loose change down the back of the sofa. When he spoke he sounded like farts. He had the charm and manners of a drunk pig feeding at the trough. He hated pretty much anyone and everything and he made no secret of trying to hide it. So it's not hard to see why he chose a career in politics.

So there you have it, that's the very short story of

Percival T. Duckholm's rise to power: he just happened to find an opponent that was even more repulsive than him. So anyway, where were we? Oh yes, Percival T. Duckholm emerged from the car. He waved and smiled at the crowds, even though no one was cheering him. In fact they were booing him. Joe looked round and saw that quite a mob had gathered. The more Percival smiled, the more they shouted and wailed at him.

'Resign, you lump!' one angry lady yelled.

'You're a crook!' another man shouted.

This just seemed to whip the reporters and cameramen into more of a frenzy. Pervical T. Duckholm ignored the crowd and headed for Mr Brooks.

'What a marvellous school you have here!' he said.

'Thank you. Would you like to meet some of the children?' Mr Brooks replied, eagerly.

'God no. It's bad enough that I have to spend time with my own!'

Joe pushed his way to the front of the crowd. This was his chance—he figured that if he just explained about the park to the Prime Minister, he would fix it—I mean, that's what Prime Ministers do, isn't it? They fix things.

15

'Er . . . Mr Prime Minister, sir, can I ask you a question?' Joe asked timidly.

'EW!' the PM shrieked. 'GET AWAY FROM ME YOU 'ORRIBLE CREATURE!'

'I just wanted to ask you a question—it's about our park . . .'

'You just wanted to fart a question about a parp?' the Prime Minister asked. 'Speak up, boy!'

'No, I wanted to ask a question about the park. Our park has been closed down, and they're going to build a big shiny tower on it.' By now, everyone was listening. Even Mr Brooks was staring at Joe, a mixture of bewilderment and anger on his face (mostly anger, maybe five per cent bewilderment). Joe wasn't used to people actually listening to him. He normally liked to sit quietly and let Ajay take the lead, but he knew this could be his only chance to save his mum's job.

'Ahhhh . . .' the Prime Minister said, smiling. 'At last, a sensible question. Yes it's true, we have closed down the grotty old park and built a shiny new tower. That's what this government is all about, building shiny new things. No need to thank me, sonny Jim!'

the PM gave Joe a toothy grin, ruffled his hair and walked away.

'What an idiot,' Ajay said, looking at the Prime Minister. 'Hey Joe, are you all right?'

But Joe wasn't all right. He was about a zillion miles from all right. His blood was hot and full of anger. How could someone so important be so useless? He felt like a fly that had just been swatted to the floor. The Prime Minister moved on, surrounded by reporters and cameramen. They were like a pack of animals, feeding on every word that fell out of his greasy mouth.

'Charlie James, World News Today. Do you have anything to say for yourself? Anything at all about the allegations that you're a crook and a thief?'

'NO COMMENT!' Percival bellowed like a fog horn in a storm.

'Do we take it from your silence that the crimes they accuse you of are true, Prime Minister?'

'Now listen here, you horrible little man!'

'Are insults the best you can do, Prime Minister?' Charlie asked, shoving the microphone right into the PM's face.

Percival T. Duckholm, clearly having had enough of being pestered, stopped in his tracks and whipped round to face the reporter.

'I know in recent days there have been several accusations about me in the newspapers. Well, I would like to say once and for all, I deny any wrong-doing. I can assure you that the huge amount of money the police found in my bank account was simply resting there until I had time to give it to the home for orphaned kittens. Furthermore, I can assure you that it was a genuine mix-up when I accidentally sold my grandmother to that travelling circus. I would also like to deny that it was me caught on camera giving those bags of cash to those dodgy businessmen—it was in fact my twin brother, that I only just discovered I had last week.

NOW GO AWAY!'

The sound of jeering and booing rose a level. The Prime Minister's pink sweat-glazed face was getting more and more irate-looking with every passing moment.

'What about the Deputy Prime Minister, Violetta Crump—do you still stand by her?' the news reporter asked. But before the Prime Minister had a chance to answer, another voice interrupted.

'Let me answer that.'

Out of the car stepped a woman dressed from head to toe in black. Her painted nails flashed in the sunlight like knives at the ends of her hands. This was Violetta Crump, the Deputy Prime Minister. She was a chilling woman, with brains as sharp as a pot of pencils dipped in lemon juice. She had a steely look on her face that made everyone feel puny and unimportant and her eyes were sly, like a snake's. The angry people were all now looking nervously at their feet, quivering.

'Do you still support the Prime Minister, Ms Crump?' Charlie James asked, his voice wobbling with fright.

'The Prime Minister and I go back a long way. He's like family to me—and one I like, not one I'd sell to a circus.'

Percival laughed nervously.

'There have been many accusations about the Prime Minister in the last few days, but I don't know why anyone would think it was *me* who told the papers about the Prime Minister's crimes—I'm sorry, his *alleged* crimes. All this talk that I'm after his job is just that, talk. Why would I want Percy's job? His big house, his power? Oh no, I'm just happy to work for such a . . . special man.' Violetta looked at Percival T. Duckholm as if he were a slug stuck on her shoe.

'Well there you have it. Violetta thinks I'm brilliant. I think I'm brilliant, now let's put this silly matter to rest. I am in charge of you lot and there's not a single thing you can do about it!'

'Oh, will you shut up, you bumbling great warthog!' came a small voice from the crowd. Mr Brooks looked round, Charlie James looked round, Violetta looked round, Ajay looked round . . . and there stood Joe, his arms folded crossly, staring at Percival T. Duckholm. There was a deathly hush.

SHOUT, SHOUT,
LET IT ALL OUT

'I do beg your pardon!' The Prime Minister snorted, his face now even redder than the reddest beetroot that there ever was. 'You again! Do you have something to say, you snivelling little wretch?'

Joe felt as though the whole world was looking at him, but for once, he didn't care.

'I said, do you have anything to say?' Percival T. Duckholm leaned in closer to Joe. He could feel the Prime Minister's hot, sticky breath on his cheek—it stank of old kippers and misery.

'Yes. Yes I do,' said Joe, trying to speak and hold his breath at the same time. 'I hadn't finished talking to you. I think you should shut up for once and try listening for a change. You . . . you big dafty!'

'DAFTY?!' Percival yelped.

'Yes. All you do is sit around in that big building, you know the one on the HP sauce bottle, all day, yawning and shouting and telling us all off.'

The Prime Minister was dumb-struck, but Joe wasn't finished yet. In fact, he'd only just started. 'All I wanted you to do was listen to me, so I could tell you about the park. Five minutes, that's all, but even that was too much to ask. All you did was shout at me and it's not right. Politicians shouldn't tell us what to do—we should tell them what to do. They work for us, don't they? We pay their wages. How can they close parks without checking with us first? The whole thing is just bonkers. And another thing . . . why do we need alarm clocks?!'

Percival T. Duckholm looked even more perplexed now. 'Alarm clocks?'

'Yes, alarm clocks.' Joe was really getting into his stride now. 'They just put people in a bad mood when they get up. Why does everything have to happen so early? If we all had a lie-in, we'd all be nicer to each other and would need fewer policemen. Then we could turn the empty jails into theme parks. But instead of being sensible and making sensible decisions, politicians just sit on big sofas all day, falling asleep and occasionally yawning "hear, hear".

'Cats should have wi-fi hubs on them! That way, everyone could get a signal all the time. Bubble-gum-blowing should be an Olympic event!' Joe paused for breath. It was as though everything that had ever popped into his head was coming out of his mouth. And he couldn't do anything about it. But the best thing was, it felt AMAZING!

'Why don't they put swimming pools on trains? It'd make journeys a lot more fun. And why do all buses look the same?' Joe suddenly asked no one in particular. 'I'll tell you why—to make us confused and late for stuff. They should have different-shaped ones for different journeys. If there was a banana bus that took you to the shops, you'd get on it, wouldn't you?' Joe said, pointing to an old gent in the crowd, who nodded enthusiastically. 'Of course you would, what sensible person wouldn't get on a bus shaped like a piece of fruit? Don't the government want people to go on buses more? Well, they should make them more interesting.

'And here's another thing—nobody under the age of fifty should ever wear a bow tie. All toilets should have electric seats to warm your bum up in the winter. There should be one day a month at school where the children get to be in charge of the teachers. Cafes should have beds instead of seats. Why do we only get to eat breakfast in bed? Shouldn't we eat every meal like that? Isn't it time we banned shows like *Britain's Got The X-Factor Voice on Ice*? Surely we have enough singers in this country now. And I would definitely, DEFINITELY make it illegal to say the word "lol". I mean, people actually say "lol" rather than just laughing! If I ever got to be in charge, things would be very different. I wouldn't waffle on about how bad the other lot had been, I'd sort stuff out. I mean, how tough can it be? Grown-ups have had their turn at running the country—why not let us kids have a go?

AT LEAST THAT WAY WE'D GET TO KEEP OUR BLOOOOOOMIN' PARKS!!!'

And JUST like that, Joe had finished, as though he'd suddenly run out of batteries. He looked around to see that everyone was staring at him, openmouthed. What seemed brilliant only a few seconds ago felt so silly now. What was he thinking? His cheeks began to flush pink with embarrassment.

Suddenly, there was a slapping sound. And then another. It sounded like—no, not sounded like, it *was*—clapping. He was being applauded!

'You tell them, son,' said one man. 'We need a few more like you in charge!'

The applause grew louder and louder. Joe looked at Ajay, Ajay looked at Joe and mouthed the word 'WOW' at him. He was stunned, but not as stunned as Joe.

Percival T. Duckholm snorted like a pig and stormed back into his car, yelling at the driver, 'Take me back now! Upstaged by a little child. I'll never hear the end of this!'

Charlie James, the TV reporter, said something to his cameraman and then turned to Joe. 'That was, you know, like totally, just, well . . . you know!'

What the heck was that supposed to mean? The TV crew whispered a few more words to each other, before making a hasty exit.

Suddenly, the realization of what Joe had done hit him like a wave of icy water.

'Do you think Mr Brooks will be mad?' Joe asked Ajay, nervously.

'What, that you just called the Prime Minister a dafty on TV? I think we're about to find out,' Ajay replied.

Mr Brooks was running after the car, banging on the window, begging Percival not to leave. And that's when Joe's eyes met Violetta Crump's. She was staring at him from the limo. She didn't blink, she didn't shout, she just stared at him. Joe felt his spine tingle, like it was made of ice-cold jelly. He grabbed his bag and headed for school, trying to look inconspicuous. The crowd parted as he walked on through the school doors down towards his classroom. Maybe it will all blow over, thought Joe as he waited for Ajay to catch him up. And that's when he sensed it. Like a deep rumble of a far-away train. A ball of anger so huge that it could be felt before it was heard. Then, like a furious belch, it hurtled out of Mr Brooks' mouth at a hundred miles an hour.

'PEEEEEEERKINS!!!!
MY OFFICE NOOOOOOW!!!'

'Wow—that was quick,' said Ajay, tapping his watch.

Joe and Ajay sat in Mr Brooks' office. They were so nervous they could barely look at each other, let alone speak. Mr Brooks bounded in, slamming the door behind him.

'I might have known it'd be you two,' he sneered. 'It's always you two.' Before Mr Brooks could utter a word of the speech he'd clearly been planning in his head, the phone started ringing. Mr Brooks picked it up and slammed it down without answering. Joe gulped.

'Mr Brooks,' Ajay started. 'I just want to say sorry, I shouldn't have . . .' He stopped mid-sentence and scratched his head. 'Hang on, I haven't done anything. Why am I here?'

'Oh, you'll be involved somewhere. You always are,' Mr Brooks hissed. The phone rang again. Mr Brooks picked it up and hung up once more without even looking away from Joe and Ajay. He was just about to start yelling again when his mobile started ringing.

'OH FOR GOODNESS' SAKE!!' he said, switching it off. 'Have you two any idea how important today was?! Our school could have been FAMOUS! Do you know what that could mean?'

'Er . . . new school books?' Joe asked.

'Eh?' Mr Brooks replied, with a note of surprise. 'Think big, lad. Wouldn't it be great if the school had a new PE block, or perhaps a new swimming pool? I was going to ask the PM for his help.'

'I just wanted him to listen about the park . . .' Joe began.

'Imagine it, Perkins. Imagine a world where the school had a private swimming pool. Only open to a very select bunch of people, know what I mean?' he said, tapping his nose.

'You mean, the children?' asked Ajay.

'Well, OK, *some* of the children. The clean ones perhaps. Maybe the kind of children who mention that their school needs a swimming pool on TV, not the kind who call the bloomin' Prime Minister a DAFTY and go on about PARKS!'

'But he is a dafty!' Joe protested.

'I KNOW THAT! THEY ALL ARE! BUT THAT'S NOT THE POINT!'

'Ohhh, I understand,' Joe said, not really understanding.

'Nothing too fancy, just one with one of those water slides, and maybe a waterfall.' Mr Brooks was still in a daydream, fantasizing about swimming pools. 'Oh, and I like those steam rooms . . . and a hot tub! But then you two blew it.'

'Once again, Mr Brooks, totally innocent here,' Ajay said, holding up his hands.

Then Ajay's phone started to ring. 'Uh oh!' Ajay gasped. 'It's for emergencies only—I never have it on during class.'

'Hand over the phone, boy!'

Ajay grabbed his phone and went to give it to Mr Brooks. 'Oh my good crikey!' he yelled, staring at the screen. 'You're not going to like this, Mr Brooks.'

Just then Ms Jones, the school secretary, burst in.

'Why aren't you answering your phone?' she cried. 'The whole place has gone berserk trying to get hold of you. I've got people from all over the world on the phone through there!'

'All over the world . . .' Mr Brooks' eyes lit up. 'Wanting to talk to me?!'

'No! They want Joe.'

'Uh, me? Why?' Joe asked, confused.

'You've gone viral!' Ajay said, handing over his phone to Joe and Mr Brooks. 'Look!'

FAME

'Viral?! Am I ill?!' Joe said with panic in his voice. 'Is it serious?!'

'No, viral, as in . . . oh, just watch!' Ajay clicked the button on his phone and it began to play.

It took Joe a second or two to realize what he was looking at, but then he made out a face. It was—yes, there was no mistaking it—it was his face!

'What the . . . what—it's me!'

'My nan in Mumbai just sent it to me!' Ajay said excitedly.

Joe was dumb-struck. His speech was being replayed before his eyes. He'd only said it half an hour ago and already he was being watched around the world! He buried his face in his hands. He'd made a fool of himself and now the whole world was watching. Joe took a peek through his fingers, expecting Ajay to be as horrified and as embarrassed as him, but he was smiling. I mean, proper big smiles. His mate was enjoying it!

'This could be big for us, Joe. We could be MILLIONAIRES!' said Ajay. 'Look how many people have watched it!'

Mr Brooks grabbed the phone. 'ONE HUNDRED AND FIFTY THOUSAND HITS!' he screamed.

'Don't be ridiculous, Mr Brooks,' snapped Ajay.

'Ohhh, phew . . . !' Joe sighed.

'That's one and a half million hits.' Ajay grinned.

It took Joe a moment to register what Ajay had just said.

'What . . . ? One and a half . . . !'

'Million!' Ajay finished off his sentence for him, grinning like a cat that not only had found the cream, but had stumbled across his own dairy. 'I mean, I know at least five of them have been my nan—look, you can see my nose in the background—but ONE AND A HALF MILLION MAAAN! Joe, are you listening to me?'

But Joe wasn't listening. He was feeling very peculiar. He sat down on the floor, as if suddenly weighed down. It had taken all his nerve to say something to the Prime Minister in the first place and now it had gone global. He didn't want any of this—he just wanted to stop the park from being closed and for his mum to keep her job.

'You're not going to throw up, are you?' Mr Brooks said, wincing. 'I don't want anyone throwing up in here.'

'Euuuuuugh . . .' Joe said. It was all he could manage.

'I know that noise, it's a throwy-up kind of a noise,' Mr Brooks said.

'Well perhaps if you stopped mentioning that word,' Ajay said crossly, 'he might not . . . you know . . . ?'

'Throw up?' Mr Brooks said.

'Amazing.' Ajay sighed.

Ajay sat next to Joe and put his arm around him.

'Joe, man, you've done nothing wrong. What you said, well it was cool.'

'I DON'T WANT TO BE COOL! COOL IS FOR OTHER PEOPLE. I WANT TO BE ME. EUUUGH!'

Joe yelled.

'OK, OK, forget cool. Forget it. But people are talking about you. Do you know what this means?'

'No, what?'

'Hmm, I'm not sure, but I think it must mean free sweets somehow! We might even get to be on TV again, or travel the world or something! But the most important thing is, this could help save the park. That's what you want, isn't it?' They both looked at each other and slowly but surely Joe began to grin. Sure, it was a 'I'm-quite-queasy-and-may-barf-at-any-moment' sort of a grin, but it was a grin all the same.

'Do you really think we could save the park?' Joe asked.

Deep in the heart of Number Ten Downing Street, a pair of grand old oak doors burst open, letting rip a crack that sent a shockwave through the building. Violetta stomped down the corridor, with a face like thunder, a phone clenched in her hand, and blood vessels popping in her forehead like rivers of hot red larva.

'I see Violetta's back,' Jenkins muttered, peering over his half-moon glasses.

Jenkins was a gentleman with an air of sophistication about him. He looked and sounded as though he was born in the wrong time, a relic from a forgotten England, a distant echo from a different age. He was old and very, very posh is what I'm basically trying to say. Jenkins was the Prime Minister's Personal Private Secretary. His job was to make sure the Prime Minister could do his. Despite his gentlemanly appearance, he was a fearsome man, with a brain so clever it was a wonder it could all fit in one head. He had the world-weary air of a man who had worked for every Prime Minister for the last forty years, and he was scared of no one. Least of all puffed-up Deputy Prime Ministers in the mood for an argument.

'WHEEEEEERE IS HE?!'

Violetta yelled, slamming her phone down on the desk so hard that one poor office worker peed his pants and had to be taken to a dark room to be rung out like a flannel. Jenkins took one last slurp of tea and folded his paper neatly away.

'Who?' he asked calmly. This seemed to enrage Violetta even more.

'LORD DUCK OF THICKHAM! Who else, you blithering idiot?' Violetta raged at Jenkins.

'Oh, the PM is just through there,' Jenkins said, nodding at a closed door. Violetta burst through into the Prime Minister's office to find the Prime Minister . . . under his desk on the phone. He hung up as soon as he saw Violetta's grisly expression.

'Now, Violetta, I can assure you that I had no idea whose luxury yacht I was sailing on the other day. I mean, if I'd known that it belonged to one of the FBI's most wanted criminals, I certainly wouldn't have gone on board.'

'Oh, shut it! Now! I haven't told the papers about that one yet, you're safe for a day or so.'

'So it was you who told them about all the other stuff!' Percival shouted, pointing his sausage finger at her face.

'Oh, you've only just figured that one out, have you, lard brain? Why didn't you just do as I said? All you had to do was get out of the car. Smile, refuse to answer questions, and tell them in a few days that you were going to resign because you were ill . . . or wanted to spend more time with your goldfish, anything! But nooooo, you couldn't even do that properly could you? We had an agreement. You hand the job over to me, you don't go to jail.'

'Sorry Violetta, please don't hurt me. I panicked— they kept asking me questions. I have my pride!'

'Coming from a man sat under a table hiding, that doesn't mean a whole lot.'

'Oh it gets much worse than that, Violetta,' Jenkins interrupted, entering the room. 'That boy— the one who called the PM a useless warthog—is all over the news. In fact he's everywhere. He seems to have achieved more popularity in two hours than you achieved in twenty years.' Jenkins began to read from a phone. '"They should make that boy PM, and get rid of Percival and Violetta" it says here. "Joe for PM, he da man", whatever that means.'

Violetta grabbed the mobile off Jenkins. 'WHAT?' She was so furious, it's no exaggeration to say her eyes went red with rage. 'It can't be. Who does he think he is?! I will not let one tiny little runt upstage me. All my life I've been waiting, always second best. Well, not anymore!'

Violetta hurled the phone at the wall where it smashed into a hundred pieces.

'What do you think of that, Jenkins?'

'Impressive. Of course it would have been more so if it wasn't your phone.'

'What?'

'I was handing you your own phone. The one you left on my desk.'

'Hahahaha!' Percival laughed.

'Oh shut up, duck features,' Violetta hissed. 'Nothing is going to stop me from becoming the next Prime Minister—not you, not him, NOTHING!'

TRANSMISSION

It had been a long day at school, long and very, very weird. All Joe wanted to do was get home and hide in his room.

'Four million, seven hundred and forty-two thousand, nine hundred and fifty-two . . . four million, seven hundred and forty-two thousand, nine hundred and seventy five . . . four million—'

'Do you have to do that?' Joe asked Ajay on their way home. Ajay had been updating Joe as the number of hits rose, and it was beginning to get on his nerves.

'Sorry. What do you think your mum will say? Do you think she'll be angry, pleased, or what?'

'I don't know. Maybe she hasn't seen it and doesn't know anything about it . . .' Joe broke off in mid-sentence as they turned the corner back into Joe's road, and were met by a scene out of some Hollywood movie set. Satellite trucks of every size and shape sat parked in the street, like big metal beasts hunting their pray. Thick cables draped across his lawn like giant black spaghetti strings weaving between each vehicle. Outside each one stood a man or woman, spluttering updates to their TV camera. Joe knew he had some explaining to do. His mum liked to watch *Countdown* at this time of day, but he was fairly certain the spectacle of half the world's TV cameras outside would be the sort of thing she'd notice.

Joe felt someone's eyes on him and turned to see a man, staring at him.

'You're him!' the old gent said, pointing at Joe.

'Am I?'

'Yeah, you know . . . you're . . . YOU . . .'

Joe found this hard to disagree with. He was him, and probably always would be.

'Him off the internet,' the man continued.

'Ohhhh . . .' Joe sighed. 'Er . . . I guess I am. Anyway, goodbye,' he said, turning round hurriedly to cross the road.

'I thought you were great,' said the man, following Joe and Ajay. 'My son got me one of those new-fangled computers a while back and I'll be honest, I loves it! You're the one person I've seen who talks sense on there.'

'Well, thanks! But I really must . . .'

'I'd vote for you, you know.'

'That's nice, but I've . . .'

'Can you sign my turnip?'

'What?' Joe stopped in his tracks and turned round.

Even Ajay was lost for words after that one.

'I've just been to the greengrocer's and I don't have any paper for an autograph, so will you sign my turnip?'

Joe shrugged his shoulders, 'Erm . . . OK, why not?'

Joe had never had to sign anything before—he didn't even have a signature. Was this how things were going to be now? Strangers thrusting vegetables at him?

'Look everyone, it's Joe!' the man hollered, beckoning other passers-by over.

'Ajay!' Joe said nervously. 'What do I do?' He wasn't used to being the centre of attention; in fact he went out of his way to avoid it at all costs. Whatever the opposite of the centre was, that's where Joe could be found.

'I dunno!' Ajay said. 'This is all pretty new to me, too. Be yourself?'

'As opposed to what? A rhinoceros wearing a hat?' Joe cried. But it was too late—the TV crews had spotted him and the journalists were running towards him. Joe gasped and screwed his eyes shut tightly. Suddenly, he felt as though he was being lifted into the air. He opened his eyes again, to see the man with the turnip, along with half the street, carrying him home as though he was a returning hero.

'JOE FOR PM!' they were all shouting. He should have felt embarrassed, but Joe couldn't help but laugh. It felt amazing!

'Joe, are you making a leadership bid?' one reporter asked.

'The whole world's talking about you—what do you make of that, Joe?' came another question.

'MY CLIENT WON'T BE MAKING ANY MORE STATEMENTS TONIGHT!' Ajay yelled.

'AJAY?!' Joe shouted, spotting him fighting his way to the front of the crowd.

'Didn't think I was going to miss out on all this fun, did you?' Ajay grinned back.

'I'm sorry, who are you?' a reporter asked Ajay.

'I am Joe Perkins' media manager, personal assistant, lifestyle guru and ping-pong partner! And if you have any questions, you'll direct them through me. Isn't that right, Joe?'

Joe looked around, drinking in the chaotic scene, took a deep breath and said, 'Yes, you heard the man. Any questions, talk to Ajay.' Joe held out his hand to Ajay. 'Welcome aboard, mate!' The two shook on it and chuckled.

'Now let's get "internet sensation" inside—he needs his tea and there's maths homework to be done,' Ajay instructed the joyful mob.

With a cheer they followed Ajay to Joe's house. They were greeted by Joe's mum, who was waiting for him on the doorstep.

'Mum, I can explain,' Joe said.

'Can you?' she asked back.

'No, not really.' Joe smiled, looking at the mob below him. 'It's been a really weird Monday. Really weird.'

'I know!' said his mum, a smile breaking across her face. 'And I'm dead proud of you, son.'

'Really!?' said Joe, climbing down from the crowd, before falling the last bit.

'Of course! You were on the TV. No Perkins has ever been on the TV before. Well, apart from your Uncle Alan, but we don't talk about him and no charges were ever brought.'

'Thank you, kind people, no more statements tonight!' Ajay said, as he ushered Joe and his mum into the house, closing the front door behind them.

'Peace at last . . .' Joe said. 'What the . . . what?!' Joe looked down the hall. Or what used to be the hall. Instead it had somehow turned into a bustling news room.

'Well, they looked cold outside, so I invited them in. Now, you can help me with the tea and marmite Swiss roll. The boys from CNN are parched. And you're just in time—I was about to get the family album out!' Mum grinned and went into the lounge.

'Family al . . . oh, bum!' Joe said under his breath.

'Excellent!' Ajay's eyes widened.

Joe walked into the lounge, which was full of TV correspondents, make-up artists, cameramen, producers, and the reporter from Joe's school, Charlie James. They were all swigging tea and chewing on Mum's scones.

'These things are tougher than gobstoppers,' a big-haired man with an American accent said.

Joe's mum grabbed the album from the cabinet, and squeezed onto the sofa, between two American journalists.

'Here's Joe when he was a little boy,' she said, passing round the photo album. 'Joe's always been a bit of a rebel—he didn't wear trousers until he was six. Look, here's the proof!'

'MUM!' Joe shrieked.

'Let me handle this,' Ajay said, stepping in like a boxing referee. 'Thank you, ladies and gentlemen of the press, I think it's about time you all went home. I've got some very important planning to do with my client.'

'Is Joe going to make a play to be Prime Minister?' Charlie asked.

'Is he after the top job?' another shouted.

'I'm a kid!' said Joe. 'Kids don't become Prime Minister! I just want to save our park!'

'No more questions please. If there's any news, you'll be the first to know!' Ajay said, settling into his new role rather too well.

The press pack muttered and grumbled but slowly began filing out of the house. Ajay grabbed Joe by the wrist and they climbed upstairs to Joe's bedroom, trying not to tread on a Korean TV crew on the stairs. Ajay slammed the bedroom door behind them. He looked at Joe and burst out laughing.

'On the scale of one to mental, this is definitely off the scale.'

'You don't think it's getting a bit out of hand, do you?' Joe said, looking out of the window at the helicopter circling above the house.

'No way, Joe! This is just the beginning.'

'This just isn't me, Ajay, this is the sort of thing you'd do. They got the wrong person,' Joe said.

'Nah, they got the right person. You just don't know it yet. You were the one who spoke up, not me. It was you who shouted at the Prime Minister so you could save the park,' Ajay said. 'Look, all this will probably blow over in a couple of days, these things always do.'

'Imagine though . . .'

'Imagine you became Prime Minister?' Ajay interrupted.

'Yeah . . . Imagine living in a big mansion, not having to go to school, or do maths homework ever again. Ice cream for breakfast, brought on a silver tray by a butler called Smithers or something! Imagine going anywhere you wanted or doing anything that you wanted!' Joe laughed.

'It would be quite a laugh, wouldn't it? Beats a paper round, anyway,' said Ajay. 'I wouldn't worry about it too much. This will all die down soon. I mean, it's not like they would let a kid become the Prime Minister, is it?'

POWER TO THE PEOPLE!

'The world of politics was thrown into chaos yesterday when a twelve-year-old boy seemed to challenge the Prime Minister's authority. Many are calling for this young lad to lead the country. That's right, a twelve-year-old boy. We're joined by constitutional expert Hugo Spivler. Hugo, could this really happen?'

'Well that's a good question, Duncan Fring. From what I can tell it doesn't say anywhere that the Prime Minister has to be a grown-up. Going through the legal documentation, it also mentions that in times of emergency, it is up to the out-going Prime

Minister to decide. If he feels that he doesn't have the support of the country, he can resign and hand over power to whomever he sees fit . . . terms and conditions apply . . .'

'Thank you, Mr Spivler. So there we have it: if the people want it, and Parliament wants it, then all the Prime Minister has to do is hand over the keys to Number Ten, as it were. It's been an extraordinary day in this country's history. It feels as though change is in the air. A change we all secretly craved but no one was brave enough to ask for. No one except Joe Perkins, a small boy with big ideas! Duncan Fring, ITV news. Back to you in the studio.'

'Oh this is just great. Just great . . .' Percival T. Duckholm sighed, watching the TV. 'I've been in politics for thirty-five years and a kid who's been doing it one day is already more popular than I will ever be. I haven't been this embarrassed since I dropped one at the state opening of Parliament.'

'Charming.' Violetta sniffed.

Percival was sitting in his office, a napkin round his neck, eating Scotch eggs, and watching the TV news. Duckholm liked to eat when he was nervous. Scotch eggs were his snack of choice and he was on his third pack.

'Do I have to do everything?' Violetta sighed.

'What?' Percival said, stuffing the first egg from bag number four into his greasy face.

'You have to offer him something. Work out what he wants and give it to him.'

'You mean offer him the . . .' Percival asked.

'Yes! He gets what he wants, you get what you want . . .'

'Well, I suppose I could . . . maybe it is time . . .' Duckholm smiled. 'Violetta, you're a genius. Let's celebrate with a Scotch egg!'

Joe woke up with a start and a thud as he fell out of bed and went about his traditional morning routine of yawning, opening the curtains, stretching, and scratching his bum.

'AAAAAARGH!'

Joe yelled, looking out of the window. There must have been close to a thousand people in the street looking up at him. Joe quickly pulled the curtains back and shook his head, trying to take in what he'd just seen. The memory of yesterday landed on his shoulders, almost making him buckle. Joe pulled back the curtain a crack and peeked out. The huge crowd below were still looking up at him. The entire street, including half the world's press, had just seen him in his

Postman Pat pyjamas, scratching his bottom. And yes, Joe knew that he was too old for Postman Pat PJs, but they were his favourite most comfortable ones and he liked to wear them. So what!

'Morning, son!' Mum said cheerfully, bursting into Joe's bedroom. 'Time to get up. I've made your favourite for breakfast.'

'I'm not hungry,' said Joe.

'All the best leaders in the world need breakfast,' Mum said sarcastically.

'I'm not Prime Minister, I am a twelve-year-old boy called Joe in Postman Pat pyjamas. All I want to do is save the park and get you your job back. I wish everyone would leave me alone and forget this Prime Minister stuff. Anyway I can't be Prime Minister today, I have double Chemistry!'

'No you don't. Mr Brooks has given you the day off. He just rang, kept muttering about a swimming pool or something. That make any sense to you?'

'Ugh . . .' Joe sighed.

'And anyway, you can become Prime Minister—the man on the news just said so. So tuck in.' Mum grinned.

'He said what now?!' Joe spluttered.

'He said if the people want it, then all the Prime Minister has to do is sign over power to you.'

'Oh well, that's not likely to happen is it, he hates me—I called him a "big dafty", remember?' Joe sighed with relief.

'Well, stranger things have happened,' Mum said. 'Now get eating, my son the big brave politician.'

'I bet the President of the United States doesn't get woken up by his mum wielding a tray of . . .' Joe looked down at his breakfast. '. . . a tray of fish and chips?'

'It's your favourite, Mr Prime Minister!' Mum said gleefully.

'For breakfast . . . ?' Joe asked, looking up at her, bewildered.

'It's your favourite, Mr Prime Minister!' Mum repeated, parrot-fashion. 'Do you want mushy peas and ketchup?'

'For. Breakfast?' Joe repeated back to her. Two can play at repeating, he thought.

'It's your—'

'Yes, yes, your favourite, Mr Prime Minister,' Joe said, finishing her sentence for her. 'Anyway, I'm not prime minister!'

'Not yet!' said Ajay bursting into Joe's room. 'Hey man, there's a six-year-old kid downstairs who wants his pyjamas back.'

'Very funny,' Joe snapped. 'Anyway, why aren't you in your school uniform?'

Ajay was wearing a suit, complete with waistcoat and tie. He had several newspapers under his arm, a mobile phone in each hand and another one tucked under his chin. He was ready for business.

'I've been given the day off too. I always liked that Mr Brooks. So chop-chop! We need to get going,' said Ajay.

'With what?' Joe said, scratching his head.

Five minutes later Joe was downstairs, dressed and with his morning hair slapped down as best he could manage. 'Right then, what's the plan?' Joe said, eating the last remaining chip on his plate that Ajay had left him.

'Well, as your media agent and lifestyle guru—' Ajay started.

'Yeah, I was thinking about that. I mean, it's great to have you on board, and don't take this the wrong way, but what do I need one for and what do you do?'

'Joe, I'm hurt. Isn't it obvious?' Ajay asked.

'Er . . .'

'You, Joe, are hot.'

'Am I?' Joe felt his forehead.

'Not hot *ill*, hot!' said Ajay. 'Hot property. Let me draw you a diagram—it's called the wheel of getting rich.' Ajay started to scribble on a napkin. 'You're famous and what we want is to be rich . . .'

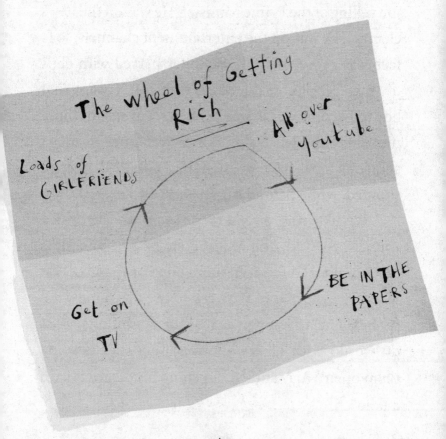

'And save the park . . . ?' Joe interrupted.

'I was coming to that . . . and to save the park . . . what we need to do is keep our options open. Perhaps a career in politics beckons, perhaps you'll just be a movie star, who knows. It's about maximizing our . . . I mean, your, potential.' Ajay flicked on the TV. Channel after channel was showing the same clip of Joe yelling at the Prime Minister. He was on the news channel, he was on the entertainment channels. Joe's face was everywhere. It was interspersed with clips of what people on the street thought. 'I want that boy to become our Prime Minister, I'm sick of those nincompoops letting us down year after year, let someone new have a go! JOE FOR PM!' a man shouted, while behind him passers-by cheered.

'It's like this on every channel on every TV round the world. You've just gone past a billion hits on YouTube. You're even more popular than that cat who plays the piano! We need to use this fame—it'll probably never happen again. The question is, what do we do with it? It's about options and keeping them open!' Ajay smiled, finishing his diagram with a flourish.

Joe sat down at the kitchen table. He looked at the newspapers that Ajay had brought round. He was on every front page. He read words like 'sensation' and 'world's most famous boy' on them, but none of it seemed to register. All he really wanted to do was save the park, yet somehow all this had happened without him even trying. Maybe that was the answer? Perhaps having no plan was the best plan? I mean, he didn't know what he was going to say to the Prime Minister yesterday, and that turned out all right . . . sort of. He could just see what happened—it's not like things could get any stranger.

Just then there was a knock at the door.

'Oh it'll be one of those autograph hunters,' Mum said, going to answer it.

'So Joe, what next?' Ajay asked.

'We have to go to Downing Street,' said Mum, coming back into the kitchen. 'That was the Prime Minister's driver at the door—Joe, you've been sent for! You don't think they're going to lock you in the Tower of London and chop off your head, do you?'

'Well now I do, yes!' Joe shrieked.

'Relax.' Ajay smiled. 'No one's going to the Tower to have their head lopped off. The most you'll do is five years in an ordinary prison. Seven years tops!'

'AAAARGH!'

Joe and his mum yelled at the same time.

'I'm KIDDING! This is good, Joe. The PM probably wants to make peace because you're making him look bad. He needs you to go away so things can get back to normal for him. He wants to offer you something . . . probably to save the park. I think you've done it, Joe. I think you've won.'

'That's all I ever wanted. And after that, we can get back to normal,' Joe said, looking at his mum. Little did he know that things would never be normal again.

HELP!

Joe, his mum and Ajay left the house via the back door to avoid the crowd, but what actually happened was a chase through the back lanes and cramped gardens of London, Joe in his best shirt, Joe's mum in her hat and coat, and Ajay in a fluster on the phone.

'No, I said *abandon* the interview. My client can't make it—he has to go to Downing Street. How many more times? Have you been drinking?! Don't you use that language at me! Oh well, that's charming isn't it? SAME TO YOU!' Ajay hung up. 'I've cancelled your appearance with Mr Tumble on CBeebies.'

A black car pulled up at the bottom of the side street. 'Perkins?' a voice from the car boomed.

'Yes!' said Joe.

'Hop in, the PM is waiting.'

'This car is bigger than our house,' Joe's mum muttered as she climbed in. The car was cool and quiet inside. The seats were black leather and more comfortable than the most comfortable sofa. It even had a TV, and not one of those ones where you can only watch a *Dr Who* DVD, but a proper telly, with all the channels.

'Hey look, it's us!' Ajay said, pointing at the screen. Sure enough, they were on TV, being filmed from the sky by a helicopter. Underneath the caption read, 'Perkins off to Downing Street for Showdown Talks.'

'Look at the crowds, Joe!' Mum squealed. The streets ahead were teeming with people. They must have all been watching the TV too, because it seemed that from every house around people were spilling out on the street to see Joe.

'We're never going to get there at this rate,' the driver said gruffly.

'Is there a sun roof . . . er . . . ?' Ajay asked.

'Stevens is the name, sir. And yes there is.'

'And there must be some sort of sound system too, right?'

'Yep. There's a speaker on the roof and a microphone in the arm rest. But it's only supposed to be used in an emergency,' Stevens added.

'This is an emergency. I've got a plan!' Ajay's eyes lit up as he lifted the mic out from its hiding place.

Slowly the sun roof opened. There was a hush from the crowds as they realized that something was about to happen. Suddenly Ajay's head and shoulders popped up clutching the microphone.

'Hello everyone!' Ajay yelled. 'Are you in the mood to break some records?'

'YEEEEES!' they all yelled with a mixture of excitement and confusion.

'Good! Here's what we're going to do. You lot go to this side of the road, and you lot to the other side.' Ajay gestured with his hands and the crowd parted down the middle, allowing room for the car to drive through. 'Now I want to see those hands, because we're about to do the world's biggest high-five-athon!' Ajay yelled. 'But you don't want just me high-fiving you, do you?'

'NO!' they all yelled.

'Who do you want?' Ajay said, cupping his hand to his ear.

'WE WANT JOE!!' they yelled in unison.

'You want whooooooooo?' Ajay's many years watching Punch and Judy shows hadn't been wasted.

'WE WANT JOE!!!' came the response, twice as loud. Ajay leant back in the car. 'Come on, Joe,' Ajay smiled. 'Let's get high-fiving!'

'I find it tricky,' Joe said, nervously. 'Last time I high-fived someone I gave them a nose bleed!'

'Oh you'll be fine, just hold your hand out. Come on, your adoring public await you.' Ajay grinned. Joe took a deep breath and poked his head out. The noise was so loud it was like someone throwing a bucket of applause all over you. At first Joe was overwhelmed, but then he looked over at Ajay and Mum, who were also hanging out of the sunroof by now, and suddenly the nerves began to melt away. 'JOE FOR PM!' everyone was yelling, over and over. Ajay, Joe and his mum all held out their hands and they high-fived the cheering crowds as they went. Joe felt a wave of happiness come over him. Not because of the limo ride of a lifetime, or the fame, but because he felt like finally he was going to win at something. He was going to see the PM to save the park and his mum's job.

A short while later the three of them arrived at Ten Downing Street. Mum and Ajay got out of the limo, followed by Joe, who lost his balance and fell out.

'We should have brought some fig rolls,' Mum said anxiously.

'Why?' Joe asked.

'You should never arrive at someone's house empty-handed,' Joe's mum insisted.

'Mrs P, we're here for showdown political talks, not a children's tea party! Right everyone, game-face on.'

'Ajay's right, Mum, let's say no to everything at first. Show them we mean business,' Joe said, determinedly.

The door of Number Ten Downing Street swung open to reveal a grey-haired gent in half-moon glasses.

'Ah, Master Perkins and family, I presume,' said Jenkins, wryly.

'NO!' Mum yelled, before grinning and nodding knowingly at Joe and Ajay.

'My mistake,' the old man said and the door slammed shut. Joe and Ajay looked at each other, then at Joe's mum. Ajay knocked on the door again. It was the same old gent.

'Hello, I'm Joe Perkins,' Joe said.

'NO HE'S NOT!' Mum yelled.

'MUM! We don't have to negotiate this bit. Let Ajay and me do the talking.'

'I'm Jenkins,' the old man said.

'NO YOU'RE NOT!' Mum yelled. 'Sorry, old habits die hard.'

Before they knew it, Jenkins had whisked them through the front door, and the hustle and bustle of outside disappeared instantly. They were standing in the hallway of a grand house, with high ceilings and plush thick carpet.

'Niiiice pad.' Ajay gave a cheeky little wolf whistle.

'Thank you, we try.' Jenkins sighed. 'The Prime Minister will see you now.'

Jenkins led the three of them down a wide corridor to a huge office. There sat Percival T. Duckholm behind a desk, with Violetta standing next to him. Duckholm chomped on his fifth Scotch egg of the day.

'Oh, *you're* here are you?' he said, spitting sausage and egg crumbs everywhere.

'Yuk, children,' Violetta sneered. 'We must get this place steam-cleaned ASAP.'

'Mr Prime Minister, sir,' Joe started, 'I just want to say, I'm sorry for losing my temper yesterday. I was just trying to save the park, you see my mum works there . . .'

'I know why you're here, and you can save me the sob stories, I've heard them a million times on

TV in the last few hours. Frankly I'm sick of the sight of you. It's not easy being Prime Minister you know. Truth be told, it's been a nightmare from day one! The coffee machine doesn't work! You'd think the Prime Minister would be able to get a decent cup of coffee wouldn't you!? And someone keeps pinching all the best choccy biscuits. I think they do it on purpose because they don't like me. I see the things they write on the toilet walls, you know: "The Prime Minister is a poo poo head"! I see them ALL! Well, stuff them, I say. I never wanted to be Prime Minister anyway, I wanted to be a train driver. Maybe I still can be? Either way, I'M OFF!!' said Percival, standing up and grinning insanely.

'What?!' Joe said.

'WHAT?' Violetta hissed.

'Here, sign this and you can have what you want.' Duckholm thrust some papers at Joe.

'You're going to save the park?!' said Joe, grabbing the papers and signing them immediately, before the Prime Minister changed his mind. Joe looked at Ajay and his mum. They'd done it, they'd won!

'What do you mean, you're off?' Violetta asked.

'I've had enough! I've had enough of him,' Percival pointed at Joe, 'and I've had enough of you!' he yelled.

Violetta tried to smile. Smiling wasn't something she'd ever really done before, but she gave it her best shot. 'Well, about time. I mean, your country thanks you for your service et cetera et cetera, but really you should have handed over power years ago.' Violetta pulled out a tape measure and started to measure the curtains. 'Well, they'll have to go for a start.'

'Wait a minute . . .' Joe muttered, looking more closely at the papers he'd just signed. 'That's not right . . . it doesn't mention anything about the park here . . .'

'I don't know why you're measuring the curtains, Violetta,' Percival said, tucking into yet another Scotch egg gleefully.

'What do you mean?' said Violetta.

'This doesn't make any sense,' Joe said, scratching his head. 'It says here that I'm the . . .'

'Because you're not going to be . . .' Percival began.

'PRIME MINISTER!' shouted Joe.

Violetta looked at Joe. Joe looked back at her. They both looked at Percival.

'WHAT?' Joe and Violetta yelled at the same time.

'You heard. Anyway, I just did as you said, Violetta. I gave him what he wanted.'

'You idiot!' Violetta shrieked. 'You've made him Prime Minister! What about me?!'

'I would have made you PM Violetta, but there was one thing that kept getting in the way.'
Percival snorted.

'What?'

'Your personality. You're a horrible person.

I mean I know I'm pretty obnoxious, but you, Violetta, are the most ghastly person that I've ever met. And I'm a politician, so as you can imagine you're up against some tough competition.'

'But I thought you were going to save the park! I thought that's why I was here!' Joe shrieked.

'Once you're PM, you can save the park. You can do whatever you want when you're Prime Minister.'

'But I don't want to be Prime Minister!' Joe cried.

'I doooooo!' Violetta cried.

'Serves you two right. Who says Percival T. Duckholm is an idiot! The only down side is I won't get to watch the fun as you two have to work together. Violetta, meet Joe, your new boss.' And with that Percival T. Duckholm started to laugh. 'And the parks? They fall under the Deputy Prime Minister's department.'

'But isn't that . . .?' Joe began.

'Joe, meet the Deputy Prime Minister, Violetta.'

Percival laughed again, only louder this time, spraying semi-digested Scotch egg everywhere. 'Have fun, you two. I'll send you a postcard from train-driver school!' and with that Percival T. Duckholm ran out of the room, tooting like a train as he went.

Joe looked down at the paper with his signature on. Perhaps Percival was joking? I mean, you know how some grown-ups think they're funny, but actually they're not. Perhaps it was one of those occasions?

'THIS CAN'T BE HAPPENING— I CAN'T BE THE PRIME MINISTER!'

Joe shouted.

'That's not what it says here,' Jenkins said, snatching the paperwork from Joe. All the colour drained from his face as he looked up solemnly at Joe. 'Welcome aboard, sir.'

LEADER OF THE PACK

'You join us outside Downing Street for what can only be described as a momentous day for the country. This is Charlie James reporting with some incredible breaking news. The Prime Minister has resigned, according to the reports we're getting, to be a train driver. In fact we have just had this short statement from Percival T. Duckhom:

'GO AWAY YOU NINCOMPOOPS, TOOT TOOT!'

TOOT
TOOT!

We are waiting for news of his successor. Will it be the Deputy Prime Minister, who we know has always harboured a dream to be PM, or could it be . . . wait . . . we're just getting word that in fact the new Prime Minister is . . . Joe Perkins. He has just signed the documents. Well I never thought I'd see a twelve-year-old boy become Prime Minister. This is a most extraordinary turn of events . . . I do believe that Joe will be coming out any moment now to say a few words.'

'I'm not going out there!' Joe panicked. 'You can't make me. I'm Prime Minister—I'll sack you. I'll sack you right now!'

'You can't sack me, I'm your mother,' Joe's mum helpfully pointed out. 'But Jenkins is right, you have to say something. The world's waiting.'

Joe sat down. Well, actually he tripped on the rug and fell down, but decided as he was on the floor anyway it would be a good time for a sit down. He looked around and saw his mum doing her best 'go on, it'll be all right' smile. The kind she did whenever Joe was in a school play, or had a swimming lesson.

'It is tradition that when one is made Prime Minister, one should say a few words to one's people.' Jenkins sighed.

'I don't want to. All I want is a sit down, and maybe have a glass of milk until all this goes away. How long am I Prime Minister for anyway?' Joe asked.

'Oh not long,' Jenkins replied.

'Oh phew . . .'

'Four, maybe five years. It'll fly by. Unless of course you do something awful and you have to resign of course . . .'

'AAAAAAARGH!'

Joe cried.

'Oh God, it's pathetic,' Violetta sneered. 'I cannot believe that that idiot has made you leader!'

'Oh, what's the big deal?' Ajay said. 'Look, you're in charge now. You can do and say whatever you like. You could go out there, sing Baa Baa Black Sheep and put your pants on your head, and nothing bad would happen.'

'Remind me again why I asked you to be my media manager?' Joe whimpered.

'I'm not suggesting you do that!' Ajay laughed, 'I mean you're Joe Perkins, the boy who can do no wrong. Just go out there and be yourself. That's why the people love you. Just tell the truth.'

'I hate to say it, but your strange little friend is right,' Jenkins chipped in.

'Thank you . . . wait, what?' Ajay replied.

'Oh, okaaaay.' Joe relented.

'I can't bear to watch this anymore,' Violetta shrieked. 'You may have won this time, but mark my

78

words, Perkins, I'll be watching you, waiting for you to fail. You've taken what's mine and I shall never let you forget it!' And with that, Violetta stormed off.

'Ignore her,' Jenkins said, mildly, as he led Joe back to the front door. 'You'll be fine, sir.'

'Call me Joe.'

'If it's OK with you, I'll stick to sir, sir.'

'Don't call me "sir sir", that's even worse!'

'But of course. Sir.'

Joe took a deep breath and stepped out to meet the waiting crowd. Joe wondered if he would ever get used to being cheered and waved at, but before he could come up with an answer he had reached the microphone. Joe stood on his tippy-toes to try to reach it, but it was no good, the stand was too high.

'It doesn't go any lower,' Jenkins whispered, suddenly at his side.

'What am I supposed to do?'

'You'll . . . you'll have to stand on my back,' Jenkins said.

'Seriously? But you must be at least eighty—I don't want to hurt you.'

'I'm sixty-two!' Jenkins hissed. 'Now just get on.'

'Oh, why not,' Joe whispered, climbing onto Jenkins' back as he knelt on all fours.

'Erm . . . hullo,' Joe said to the expectant crowd. He cleared his throat, nervously. 'So it seems I'm the new Prime Minister then. Not really sure how that happened. I think my first job as Prime Minister is to read everything I sign, really, really carefully.'

There were a few chuckles from the crowd.

'Thank the previous Prime Minister. It's a tradition!' Jenkins hissed from below.

'Oh right, yeah.' Joe nodded, trying to control the wobble in his voice. 'I would just like to take a moment to thank the previous Prime Minister for all his hard work. I know that he will be a big loss to the Scotch egg manufacturers of Great Britain.' There were a few more chuckles from the crowd. Joe turned round, and his mum gave him a big smile and a big thumbs up. He was starting to get into his stride now. 'And I think we all wish him well in his new career as a train driver. I would like to thank my mum and Ajay because without them, I wouldn't be here.' Ajay and Joe's mum grinned at each other.

'The last few days have been very odd. I mean, I should be in double Chemistry, but instead I'm about to take charge of the country. I've never even had a paper round before, so who knows how it'll go?'

Joe stopped to take in the crowd. This was his chance to do something. To make a difference.

'One thing I promise you is that it won't be dull, and I shall do my best by this country and its people!

Where there is grumpiness, may we bring giggles, where there is jelly, may we bring ice cream, where there are chairs, may we bring whoopee cushions! Thank you and goodbye!' There was a squeal of feedback from the mic and a squeal from Jenkins as Joe jumped down. Then a huge cheer broke out. There was no going back now. Joe was Prime Minister. Joe was in charge of the whole country. And do you know what? It sort of felt good!

'I can't believe they've put a *child* in charge of the country. Never in all my days have I seen anything like this,' Jenkins said to himself, wiping a single tear from his eye.

'It's a historic day, eh. Feeling kinda emotional?' Joe said, noticing the now sobbing Jenkins.

'Something like that, sir.' Jenkins dabbed his eye with a hanky and let out a howl of anguish before regaining his composure. 'Downing Street is big enough for all of you and we can arrange to move your family in tomorrow. Perhaps sir would like a tour of his new Prime Minister's residence?'

OUR HOUSE

'Welcome to your new home,' Jenkins said drily, handing Joe a mobile phone. 'Every PM gets a Prime Ministerial phone. It has all the latest technology, camera, and recording facilities. This house is the beating heart of Britain. Every decision about the country for the last few hundred years all comes from here.'

There was a hum to the place, the sound of people talking and the tapping of fingers on keyboards. It felt busy, as though behind every corner there was something hugely important and secretive going on.

The whole place had a strange . . . not feel, exactly
. . . more like a smell. It lingered in the nose and
stuck to the back of the throat. What was it?
Joe sniffed loudly.

'What is that smell?' he asked.

'Don't look at me,' Ajay said innocently. For once
it wasn't Ajay. It was something else. Joe shook his
head, puzzled, and carried on following Jenkins.

'Oh look, they've got a downstairs lav!' Joe's mum
said, rather too loudly for Joe's liking.

'Actually, we have thirty-eight,' Jenkins said.

'Blimey. Told you it'd be posh,' said Mum.

Joe stopped in his tracks, in awe of the sight
before him. They were standing at the foot of a giant

Lord Whiffy

staircase which twisted up to the top
of the house. There were photographs
all the way up the wall. Joe liked how
they started in black and white and
moved into colour, the higher he
looked.

'Whoah! That's all the Prime
Ministers there's ever been, right?'

Ajay asked, impressed.

'Will I get my picture put up there too?' Joe breathed.

'But of course, Prime Minister.'

Paul Mifinger

The first time anyone had actually called him 'Prime Minister'. Joe felt a mixture of excitement and nerves swirl round his belly.

Sir Henry Spam

'And now for the tour.' Jenkins had clearly given this speech once or twice before. 'Ten Downing Street has been the home of the Prime Minister since 1732. It contains roughly a hundred rooms, give or take a broom cupboard or two.' It was a job for Joe, Mum and Ajay to keep up as Jenkins strode down the main corridor highlighting various points of interest. The rooms were huge, the biggest Joe had ever seen. Suddenly Joe felt very small indeed. Joe and Ajay noticed something else too. People were poking their heads out of rooms and round walls to stare at them.

'I feel like we're in a zoo,' Ajay whispered.

'I know, I don't know whether to wave or growl!' said Joe.

'It's him!' Joe heard on more than one occasion.

'Who are all these people?' Joe asked Jenkins.

'These are your staff, Prime Minister,' Jenkins replied. 'They are here to help and advise you.Running a country is a huge undertaking and one person can't do it on their own. For instance, sir,' Jenkins stopped and at the top of his voice barked 'WHAT'S THE VALUE OF THE AMERICAN DOLLAR AGAINST THE POUND?'

From nowhere, a head popped round a door. '1.6018!'

'Ooh, can I try?' Joe asked eagerly.

'I don't see why not,' Jenkins said, wearily.

'HOW LONG'S A PIECE OF STRING?' Joe yelled at the top of his voice.

'AN AVERAGE OF 1.574 METRES LONG,' a voice from upstairs called down.

'WHAT'S THE MOST POPULAR FLA-VOUR OF MILKSHAKE?' Ajay joined in.

'STRAWBERRY . . .' came the far off answer, '. . . BUT PERSONALLY I LIKE CHOCOLATE.'

'They're good, aren't they?!' Joe was astonished.

'They're the best, Prime Minister,' Jenkins answered. 'Shall we move on?' Jenkins pushed open another door, to a huge room with a big table in the centre.

'This is the cabinet room,' Jenkins announced. 'The most important room in the whole house. This is where you'll make all your biggest decisions.'

'Like saving the park?' Joe asked.

'Indeed,' Jenkins replied.

Joe twitched his nose again. He could still smell that smell. What on earth was it? It was beginning to drive him mad.

'There's also a private garden that only you have access to, as well as living quarters. The house comes complete with three hundred members of staff, including butlers and cooks.'

'I don't know what to say . . . you could fit a roller

coaster in there,' said Joe, staring out into the garden. 'I'll take it!'

'Normally a Prime Minister likes to decorate several rooms in his or her own taste. Would that be of interest to you, Prime Minister?' Jenkins asked.

Joe looked at Ajay. Ajay looked at Joe. Their eyes sparkled with delight.

An hour later, Jenkins was standing next to a huge flipchart showing plans of each and every room.

His ankles were buried under scrunched up pieces of paper. Sweat rolled down his face.

'Are we all finally agreed? You want a fast-food bar, complete with arcade and laser quest in the basement. A jelly room, for any, quote "jelly emergencies" end quote. A movie room, along with a choc-ice seller on stand-by at all times. A fireman's pole. I can ask about a shark tank but I have a feeling health and safety will say no. You want a room set aside for every new toy that's invented and you want me to ask about a theme park in the back garden?'

electric pants

Burger Bar
SHARKS!
Jelly room

Joe and Ajay looked at each other and replied together, 'Yes!'

'Leave it with me, PM. Now you should really think about going to your office and taking some calls—it's traditional for world leaders to phone you and congratulate you on being the Prime Minister. They should be calling any second.'

'How long will that take?'

'Well, there are over two hundred of them, so five hours should cover it,' came a voice from down the corridor, round the corner and up the stairs.

'TWO HUNDRED! FIVE HOURS?'

'I'm sorry sir, it *is* usual,' Jenkins replied.

'I've got a better idea,' Joe said in his best plotting voice.

'Hello, Prime Minister, my name is Jim James III, President of the United States. I'm just ringing to congratulate you on your victory.'

''Ello Mr President, sir, I'm afraid the Prime Minister can't come to the phone as he has a spot of Maths homework to finish off. This is his mother.'

Joe gave her a big thumbs up.

'Oh . . . well, it's nice to meet you, ma'am,' the President replied.

'What's the weather like where you are? It's a bit parky out today.'

'Parky? Er . . . the weather's fine here, ma'am.'

'Oh, call me Doreen. Tell me, where's some good places to visit in America? I fancy going out there for my fiftieth next year. I want to go shopping in New York, like on the films. Tell me, do you have M&S over there?'

Mum put her hand over the receiver, grinned and nodded, 'It's nice to have a nice sit-down and a nice chat isn't it?'

'Only another 167 to go!' Joe said.

'Oooh, you better put the kettle on.'

Joe chuckled and closed the door on his mum.

'Settling in . . . Prime Minister?' Joe turned round to see Violetta stalking towards him, Ajay and Jenkins. Joe decided that he was going to be pleasant. Very pleasant indeed. He gave her a warm grin and stretched his hand out. 'No hard feelings?' he said to Violetta.

'Of course not. I'm sure your time here will be . . .

memorable,' she said, trying that smile again. 'In the same way that falling off a cliff or having your arm chewed off by a rat is memorable.'

Joe withdrew his arm, fast.

'Oh I'm sorry—did you think that grown-ups were supposed to be nice to children? How terribly bad of me to disappoint you. The thing is, this isn't a game, this is real, and you'll soon find out that grown-ups don't play fair AT ALL.'

Joe stared at her. He was determined to keep his composure. 'We'll see who wins in the end,' he said, managing a smile that was almost genuine.

'That smell? The one that's been bothering you since you walked through the door? That, my boy, is the smell of power, and it belongs to me, so don't get used to it.' Violetta turned on her heel and stormed off.

'Don't worry Joe, you're PM now. That pretty much means you can do anything you like. You could probably have her exterminated or turned into sausages or something, right Jenkins?' Ajay said, winking.

'Definitely not!' Jenkins exclaimed.

'Oh right, I get it, "definitely not",' Ajay said, doing air quotes with his hands and winking and nodding at Jenkins.

'Stop winking at me! You can't have anyone killed and turned into sausages.'

'No, no, I totally get it man!' Ajay said, tapping his nose.

'Will you STOP that!'

'Stop what?'

'Winking! And tapping your nose!' Jenkins pinched the bridge of his nose with his fingers and sighed. 'It's been a long day. I suggest you retire for the night. Tomorrow is your first cabinet meeting so I would advise that you get some sleep. I took the liberty of speaking to Ajay's mother earlier, and she is happy for him to stay over if that suits the both of you?'

Ajay and Joe looked at each other.

'SLEEEEEP OVEEEEER!'

They both yelled together and went for a high-five. Sadly, Joe missed and caught Ajay on the nose.

CHAIRMAN OF THE BOARD

Next morning landed with a thud as Joe fell out of bed, once again. He scratched his head. What was that noise? Joe opened the window on a group of workmen drilling, and shouting instructions to each other, while a big yellow digger dug and shifted huge piles of dirt in the garden.

'Would you mind keeping it down?' Joe asked.

'Sorry lad, some clown's got us building a rollercoaster in the garden!'

'Oh, er . . . you carry on then,' he said, closing the window.

Joe yawned and gazed across the plush bedroom. I could get used to this, he thought.

'MORE CHIPS!' Ajay shouted in his sleep, waking himself up.

'You had enough chips last night,' Joe said, looking down at Ajay on a camp bed next to Joe's huge four-poster.

There was a knock at the door, and Jenkins entered. 'Prime Minister, you must get dressed—the cabinet meeting is about to start.'

'Of course, I need to save the park!' said Joe.

'It's not just about the park, sir, it's about running the country.'

'I guess . . . but what else should I do?' Joe whispered.

'Pass some laws? That's usually how it goes,' Jenkins said, sighing with exasperation.

'Laws . . .' Joe looked at Ajay, smiling. 'Oh yeah, we'll pass some laws!' And they both began to laugh hysterically.

The cabinet room was packed. There were thirty or so men and women crammed in, all staring at Joe a little apprehensively.

'Good morning, ministers,' Joe said, grinning.

'Good . . . morning . . . Prime . . . Minister,' they all said back at him in that slow robotic way kids do in assembly. Joe was starting to get used to being called Prime Minister, even though it still made him giggle a bit inside.

It's worth pointing out at this point what a

minister actually is. It's a posh name for a person who works for the Prime Minister. The Prime Minister is the person in charge of the ministers. Forgive me if you know all this, but it never hurts to explain things does it? Say for instance you wanted to do something about schools—say for some reason you wanted a day when the teachers get to be the pupils and the pupils get to be the teachers, I don't know . . . every month. Then you'd get the Education Minister to figure out all the details (that's code for getting the poor sap to do all the work) and if it's a success, the Prime Minister takes the credit, and if it doesn't, well just blame the minister in charge. That is, in essence, how government works. Now, where were we . . . oh yes, first day of school . . . I mean first day of cabinet.

'Can I just say on behalf of all of us, we are delighted to have you as our new leader,' said a slimy-haired, pasty-faced man near the front (by pasty, I mean he had a pale face, he did not have a face like a hot meaty snack).

'Thanks! And who are you?' Joe asked.

'My name's George Unwin, I am First Lord Chancellor of the Exchequer.'

'Say what now?' Joe enquired.

George Unwin looked more than a bit put out. He was a man not used to being unknown. There were a few sniggers from other ministers.

'Is something funny?' Joe asked, innocently.

'Sorry, Prime Minister, sir, it was Darcey from Environment,' said another minister, pointing to a lady with hair so big it looked as though it had been sculpted out of a hedgerow.

'You snitch, Peters. You were laughing too,' she snarled.

'Hush now, or you'll all have to stay in when it's play time,' Joe joked.

Jenkins whispered something in Joe's ear.

'What?!' Joe said. 'I've just been informed that you don't get play time. Well, I say we have morning play, afternoon play and lunch play.' Joe looked around the room. 'Can someone make that into a law please?'

'Already done it!' came a far off distant voice from down the corridor.

'Now, where were we? Oh yes, Lord of the Checkers . . . what do you do?'

'Exchequer! . . . Sir,' George Unwin said, desperately trying not to shout, before sighing and adding, 'it means I'm in charge of the money.'

Ajay whispered something in Joe's ear.

'Roll around in it naked, you say . . . ?' Joe asked Ajay, just to be sure he hadn't misheard.

Ajay nodded.

'OK. Ajay and I would like to see the money if that's OK—we want to . . . erm . . . you know . . . just check it's all there.'

'Well, I don't have it on me!' the Chancellor said.

'Obviously!' Joe said. 'I'm not an idiot. So where is it? In your office, under your bed?' Joe laughed.

'Well, no . . . it's . . . you know . . . it's . . .'

'You don't know, do you?' Joe had stopped smiling now.

'Yes, of course I do, it's in the bank, probably, somewhere,' Unwin said, his face slick with sweat.

'Look, if you don't know where all the cash is, just say. You can be honest,' Joe insisted.

'No . . . I'm sure I do know where it is . . . I think . . . Actually, I don't know where it all is,' he said, scratching his head. 'Would it be OK if I just popped out to . . . go and check we haven't lost all the money?'

Joe nodded, casually. 'Probably a good idea.'

'Anybody else need to go and find anything? Check we haven't lost track of any battle ships, misplaced a hospital or three, accidentally dropped a couple of prisons down the back of the sofa?' Several ministers, desperate not to catch anyone's eye, tip-toed out after George Unwin.

'Right,' said Joe, clapping his hands. 'Let's get started. My name is Joe, I am your Prime Minister. Super excited about that, obviously. First thing—let's get a few laws going shall we? We have playtime for

100

ministers now, all those in favour of expanding it to everyone, raise your arm. Good,' Joe said without even bothering to do a count. 'Also, I say we have a fancy dress day at least once a week. People in suits always look so sad, let's have a "Fancy Dress Friday", but on a Thursday. I think jelly should be free on the NHS and let's make it illegal to have those comb-over haircuts—you know, the ones where people have clearly gone bald, but yet they insist on combing their hair right over the top of their shiny head.'

At this point several members of the cabinet put their hand over their own heads trying to hide their awful comb-overs.

'I think we should have one day a month where the teachers get to be the pupils and the pupils get to be the teachers. Let's start that tomorrow!' Joe grinned. 'I'd like to fund research into finding out once and for all what happens to odd socks—it's, and I think I can speak for everyone, a problem that has blighted society for far too long. I suggest we replace the handshake with the more modern high-five and have more dogs hanging out of car windows. If we could get that policy rolling out as soon as possible too, that would be great. And I'd also like to expand Britain's space programme to include sending a cow to Venus. If we don't do it, someone else will. And last but not least I want to save the park by my house. Well, not just that one but all the parks. Who's in charge of parks again . . . ?'

The door creaked open and Violetta walked in. Joe watched the atmosphere in the room suddenly shift, as if someone had turned a dial from 'lovely and happy' to 'eek!'.

'That would be me,' Violetta said, raising her eyebrow.

'Oh, yeah, how could I forget? Well, Violetta— can I call you Violetta?'

'No.'

'Well, what do I call you?' Joe asked. Ajay whispered something unrepeatable in a children's book into Joe's ear.

'You can call me "Crump",' Violetta snarled.

'Very well . . . Crump . . . now I know you and I have our differences, but what say we put those aside and see if we can . . . you know . . .' Joe gulped, 'work together, like friends . . . ?'

'Friends are for idiots. Parks are for kids. Why on earth would I want to save parks when they can be sold for cash?'

'Well, parks are fun,' Ajay said.

'Who cares about fun?!' Violetta seethed.

'I DO!' said Joe. 'In fact I think everyone should have as much fun as possible. I mean, why is it only kids that play in parks? Why don't we have special swings and slides for grown-ups too? Let's make it a new law. I'm talking bouncy castles for pensioners, climbing frames for firefighters, big twizzly slides for hot-shot lawyers. We should have a big reopening of the park. LET'S DO IT!'

Everyone in the room nodded and smiled enthusiastically, apart from Violetta.

'Now you want grown-ups having fun too!' she sneered.

'I take it you're not in favour of my idea,' Joe sighed. 'But you are forgetting that I am Prime Minister, so I can sort of save the park anyway.'

The room shifted uneasily. No one had ever stood up to Violetta Crump before. The whole room held its breath and waited for her to explode. But she didn't. She didn't say a word. She just smiled (well I say smile, her mouth went pointy at the corners, it was as close to smiling as she could get).

'We'll see,' she said as she left the cabinet room.

'That's settled then. When can we open the park?' Joe asked.

'It's going to take a few days to arrange,' Jenkins said.

'Let's have a big ceremony! You know, invite the press, have someone special to do the honours—in fact, I know the perfect person to declare the park open!' Joe grinned.

'Consider it done, Prime Minister,' Jenkins said, looking at his watch and then saying something quietly to Joe.

'Cabinet dismissed!' Joe shouted, looking at Jenkins in amazement. 'Go enjoy your play time, you've earned it!'

Joe turned to Ajay. 'We're going to meet the Queen!'

DON'T STOP ME NOW

It was a short drive from Downing Street to Buckingham Palace, but it was just long enough to be given a pep-talk by Jenkins.

'It's important that you know a few rules about how to behave when in the company of the Queen. Bow from the neck, not from the waist, call her "Your Majesty" the first time you meet her, then call her "ma'am". Remember, it's ma'am that rhymes with jam, not ma'am that rhymes with arm. Never turn your back on her or she'll—'

'Karate chop you in the kidneys?!' Ajay laughed, as did everyone else in the car.

'No!'

'Stick up her fingers in a very rude way?' Joe joined in.

'Oh, what's the point . . .' sighed Jenkins.

'Relax, Jenkins, we won't let you down, everything's going to be all right,' Joe said calmly.

The limo swept through the palace gates and into the courtyard, where two soldiers saluted as they went by. The car slowed to a halt, trumpet players began a fanfare, and footmen and butlers lined up outside the front door.

'Welcome to the palace, Prime Minister. I'm Simpkins,' said a bespectacled man, opening the car door for them.

'Look, Jenkins, the palace has got someone just like you,' Joe said, smiling.

'I'll see you back at Downing Street, sir,' Jenkins said, shaking his head. 'Behave, and don't be surprised if she's not what you expected. She can be a little . . . eccentric at times.'

'Eccentric? What do you mean?' Joe called after

Jenkins, but it was too late, the limo was already speeding off back towards Downing Street.

'The Queen is ready for you, Prime Minister.' Simpkins led them to a huge pair of doors. 'Her Majesty will see you now.'

Joe took a deep breath and went in, followed by Ajay.

'SHHHHHHHH!'

Joe looked at Ajay in alarm. Where was the voice coming from? Slowly, from behind a curtain, emerged the Queen. On a pair of roller skates.

She had curlers in her hair and a huge catapult in her hand. She pulled back the elastic and—

TWAAAAAAAANG!

The shrill noise sliced through the room. The pellet shot through the window.

'BLOOMING PIGEONS! Coming round here, nibbling on my nuts. Those are for REAL BIRDS!' she yelled at a flock of startled pigeons.

'HA! GOT YOU, YOU LITTLE FLYING RAT!!'

The Queen put her catapult down, satisfied.

'Who are you? Have you come about the moles?' she asked, looking Joe up and down.

'No, Your . . .' Joe couldn't remember the rules, something about jam arms? 'No, Your Queeniness . . . I'm the Prime Minister.'

'Oh, of course you are! My mistake, come here and let's high-five!!! Much more exciting than those boring old handshakes, wouldn't you say?' The Queen gave Joe a high-five and Ajay a fist-bump. 'Now I guess you know why you're here, it's to tell me what's going on in the world. You'll be the ninth Prime Minister I've worked with, and I'll be honest, most of them are idiots and the rest plain weird.'

The Queen shot across the room on her skates backwards, pulling back her catapult and taking another shot out of the window, before skating round the table back to where she had started. 'Got you, you little stinker!' she yelled happily. 'Now, where was I? Oh yes, most of them are weird. But you, my lad, I like you.'

'Wow . . . er . . . I mean, thank you, Your . . .' Joe smiled.

'Queeniness?'

'Yes, Your Queeniness. Well, I have a few plans

for the country, to keep people happy. Dressing up every week, swimming pools on trains, reopening parks, that sort of thing.'

'Quite right my lad . . . but what about this Crump person?' the Queen asked sincerely. 'She seems terribly grumpy and quite rude. I'd watch your back if I were you.'

'Oh, I dealt with her. She won't be any trouble,' Joe said confidently.

'Really? Sometimes one thinks one's dealt with a problem and it comes back to bite one on one's bum.' The queen grabbed Joe's hand and looked into his eyes. 'Do you know how I know?'

'Years of diplomacy, Your Queeniness? Decades of talking to Prime Ministers and world leaders?'

'Oh no, dealing with those bloomin' pigeons!' she laughed.

'Good morning, I'm Cuthbert Dwibble and this is the news. You may well be wondering why I'm wearing a tiara and a leather mini-skirt. Have I gone bananas? No, of course not, I am Wonder Woman. Well it is

Thursday, so that can only mean one thing: it's Fancy Dress Friday. One of the many new laws that our new Prime Minister, Joe Perkins, has introduced. We're joined by Charlie James outside Downing Street. Over to you, Charlie—excellent costume there, I see you've come dressed as a homeless person.'

'Actually, I didn't have time to find a fancy-dress costume. These are just my clothes. But thank you anyway, Cuthbert . . . thanks a lot . . . Yes that's right, it's Joe Perkins' first month in charge and what an impact he's made. It's like waking up in a different country. And not just here—all over the world, there are reports of fancy-dress days breaking out across the globe. It seems that the Prime Minister can't do any wrong! I caught up with him and got a few words earlier.'

Joe burst out of Number Ten, cowboy hat on and swinging a lasso.

he yelled.

Charlie James pushed the microphone right up to Joe's nose. 'Prime Minister, how have your first few days in charge been?'

'Well, I sure am glad you asked me that, partner!' Joe said in his best cowboy voice. 'It's been pretty rootin' tootin' good, I feel I'm really getting a . . . no, it's no good, I can't keep the accent up . . . handle on things.' Joe finished his sentence in his normal voice. 'I've introduced a whole host of new laws to make Britain fun again. I'm getting serious about silliness, Charlie. And I'm not afraid to take on the big issues affecting people in their everyday lives. I'm introducing a new law that gives everyone a free ice cream on hot days as well as fast-tracking my hats-for-cats scheme.'

'Hats for cats, what's that?'

'It's basically putting hats on cats, Charlie, don't need to over-think that one. Not only do cats look good in hats, but it also rhymes, which is very pleasing.'

'Prime Minister, can you confirm rumours about clogs on frogs or gloves on doves?!' another reporter jumped in.

'All in good time.' Joe smiled.

'What about the park? I mean that was the whole reason you got into politics in the first place?' Charlie asked.

'I can confirm that the park will be reopening in a few days. We're going to have a special cere-mony and a surprise guest to open the whole thing!' Joe grinned.

Ajay emerged from Number Ten, dressed in glasses, a grey wig and pink tie.

'Ah, here's my partner now . . .' Joe said, attempting the accent once more. 'Now if you'll excuse me we have to pay a visit to my old school. It's the first teacher/child swap day and I want to see it for myself.'

Joe and Ajay headed for the car. Jenkins was already waiting inside, holding a stack of papers for Joe to sign.

'Excellent costume, Ajay. Let me guess. Charles Dickens?' Joe said, climbing in.

'No!' Ajay shook his head.

'Hmmm, the Duke of Wellington?'

'No!'

'The man who invented the steam train, Robert . . . Louis . . . Armstrong?'

'Wrong again!' said Ajay.

'Ridiculous spotty tie, old-fashioned clothes . . . strange little glasses . . . no, I give up,' said Joe.

'I've come as Jenkins!'

'Ha! Of course, I see it now.' Joe laughed.

'I beg your pardon?' Jenkins exclaimed. 'I do not dress like that!'

'You sort of do. It's a good look—I mean, you just don't see enough men in pink spotty ties anymore. It's tragic really,' Joe said, kindly.

'I might start dressing like this every day from now on,' Ajay said, checking himself out in the rear-view mirror.

'Anyway, where's your costume Jenksy, why aren't you taking part?' Joe asked.

'Actually, sir, I am taking part. The more discerning observer would notice that I usually wear a Windsor knot in my tie. Well not today—I've gone for the far more relaxed standard variation. No one can accuse me of being a stick in the mud,' Jenkins said, with an air of triumph in his voice.

'Quite so, Jenkins, quite so,' said Joe, sharing a smile with Ajay.

Joe gently tapped the glass that separated the driver from his passengers. 'To St Peter's School, Stevens. Time's getting on!'

'Sorry, Prime Minister, the traffic is chaos—we'll never make it through London at this rate. Nothing I can do, your PM-shipness.'

'Oh, man,' Joe said, slumping down in his chair.

'If only we had jet packs . . .' Ajay muttered as he stared out of the window.

'Hmmm, yesssss . . . if only . . . hmmmmm . . .' Jenkins said to no one in particular. There was something about his voice that stuck in Joe's ear. Something about the way he sat on his hands that alerted Ajay. They both looked at him.

'Jenkins?' Joe asked suspiciously.

'Hmm, yes?' Jenkins asked innocently.

'Anything I should know?'

'No, absolutely not, we definitely, definitely don't have any jet packs at Number Ten.'

'We do have jet packs, don't we, Jenkins?'

Jenkins let out a desperate sigh. 'Yes. But they're for emergencies only. No Prime Minister has ever used one. It's not the polite way to get about, sir. Far too noisy and extravagant.'

Joe banged his fist on the window to the driver. 'STEVENS, TURN THIS CAR AROUND! From now on, Jenkins,' Joe leaned in, 'I shall only ever travel by jet pack!' Ajay whooped and Jenkins wept into his spotty tie.

A few minutes later all three of them were strapped in and ready to fly. Joe had stuck a crash helmet over his cowboy hat, and Ajay and Jenkins looked like inter-galactic father and son spacemen in their matching suits and goggles.

'Let's fire them up, on three . . . two . . . one . . . go!' shouted Joe. And with that all three of them rocketed into the air from the back of Downing Street.

'PRIME MINISTER ON A JET PACK!' yelled one passer-by.

Joe looked down and gave a salute. It was an amazing feeling seeing London disappear under their feet, and within seconds the whole place looked like a miniature model village, filled with toy cars and tiny robot people all crawling around in fancy dress.Joe turned to Jenkins, who still hadn't opened his eyes. 'How do you fly one of these things?'

'HOW ON EARTH SHOULD I KNOW!' Jenkins yelled, eyes still tightly closed.

'I thought you knew everything!' Joe yelled back. Suddenly the ground seemed very far away.

'Do I look like a man who flies around on a jet pack a lot?! Hmmm, do I? I'm nearly sixty-three years old. I feel dizzy if I get out of a chair too quickly! The closest I get to extreme sports is doing my tie in a slightly different way, so why on earth would you think I know how to fly a jet pack!'

'Relax, you two.' Ajay looped the loop around them. 'It's easy. This lever is for forwards and backwards, this for up and down.' And with that, Ajay zoomed off again, determined to write his name in the sky.

After a moment of uncertainty, Joe and Jenkins began to get used to being in the air.

'Hey, this isn't so bad is it?' Joe called to Jenkins.

'I suppose not.' Jenkins opened one eye and looked around. 'Just as long as we keep an eye out for any . . .'

'JUMBO JET!' Ajay yelled, just as a Boeing 747 coming into land flew within what felt like inches of their heads.

SCHOOL'S OUT

After circling the school field a couple of times they landed with all the grace of a swan landing on a still pond. Well, one of them did. Joe crash-landed into a bush and Jenkins landed in a tree with all the style of a cannon ball.

'One moment Jenkins, we'll get you down!' Joe said, staggering upright and pulling off his crash helmet to reveal what can only be described as some spectacular helmet hair.

'Oh leave me, sir. You two go on,' Jenkins muttered, breathlessly. 'I'll just stay here and have a rest. It will give me a chance to reflect on where my life went so wrong.'

'Right you are! We'll be back in an hour to take you home. Try not to get eaten by squirrels.'

By now a large crowd of pupils had gathered in the school field and Joe and Ajay were greeted like rock stars.

Joe held his arms aloft in an attempt to quieten the crowd. 'Fellow kids of the world. As you know, this is an important day in the history of our country. A day in which you get to be in charge of the teachers. We get to show them that having fun is as important as doing lessons. Good luck comrades, and let the entertainment begin!'

It was hard to believe that only a few days ago Joe was too shy to even put his hand up in class. Now he was talking to hundreds of people without even thinking about it. Joe couldn't work out if he'd changed, or if this was the real him.

Mr Brooks came scurrying on to the field with a look of wild terror in his eyes.

'Ahhh, Prime Minister, how wonderful for you

to join us on this . . . special day,' Mr Brooks said with a forced smile. 'You're just in time for . . . in fact, what are we doing today?'

'Have you asked your pupils? That is kind of the point,' said Joe.

'No. Oh, what a good idea.' Mr Brooks' sarcasm dial had been turned all the way up to eleven.

'Any suggestions about what to do today?' Ajay shouted to the pupils.

'We could make stink bombs in science!' one boy shouted out.

'Excellent.' Joe smiled.

'How about reading comics in English?' a girl yelled.

'Brilliant! And what about this morning?' Joe asked.

'We normally have PE,' Mr Brooks said, then, 'Oops,' realizing that it was probably a mistake to open his mouth.

'Even better!' Joe grinned. 'How about a game— teacher versus pupils! What shall we play?'

'Football!' someone yelled.

'No, netball!' someone else shouted.

'No, cricket!' another said.

'That settles it! We'll have a game of SOCCERNETCRICKETBALL!'

Everyone apart from Mr Brooks cheered madly.

'But I don't have my games kit!' Mr Brooks said. Joe and Ajay shot him a glance. 'No!' Mr Brooks protested. 'It's undignified!'

'You know the rules.' Joe shrugged.

Ten minutes later, the entire teaching staff were on the field.

There was Mrs Sanderson, the elderly home economics teacher; Mr Pop, the eccentric maths teacher, who blinked and grinned in the bright sunshine, as though this was the first time he'd ever been on a sports field in his life; and Mr Peters, the PE teacher, who was busying himself doing all kinds of complicated stretching exercises. They were all dressed in what could be scavenged from the lost-property box. All except Mr Brooks, who had been made to do PE

in his pants and vest. At either end of the field there were two netball hoops, and in between them, three hundred very excitable students. Ajay had assigned himself referee.

'ARE WE READY?!' Ajay yelled.

'But what are the rules?' Mr Brooks asked.

'I don't know', Ajay smiled.

'But you're the referee! Surely there must be rules. Everyone needs rules—rules are good. Rules are safe!'

'Let's just start and see what happens,' said Ajay, grinning and wiggling his eyebrows up and down.

'I hate this game already!' Mr Brooks sighed. Ajay raised his arms and blew his whistle.

PEEEEEEP!

Joe ran from the middle of the field with the ball and charged towards the net, screaming at the top of his voice.

'WHHHHHHHAAAAAAA!'

'Hand ball!' Mr Brooks yelled.

'Yellow card!' Ajay shouted.

'Ha!'

'Yellow card to you, Mr Brooks!'

'What for?'

'Telling the ref what to do. Any more of that and you'll have to do a forfeit.'

Meanwhile Joe was hurtling towards the net, the ball tucked under his arm. He had his mind on only one thing—a hoop goal. Suddenly, out of the corner of his eye a blur flashed towards him. The next thing Joe felt was the air being forced from his lungs as he was knocked to the ground in a heap. Mrs Sanderson, a woman who must have been in her seventies, had full-on rugby-tackled Joe, causing him to spill the ball.

'IN YOUR FACE!' she screamed at Joe, before walloping the ball upfield. 'I mean, hard luck, Prime Minister.'

'Good tackle, Mrs S,' Joe smiled, pulling himself to his feet. The ball hurtled towards Mr Brooks. He was just about to hit it with his cricket bat when he looked up and noticed three hundred of his students charging his way. Mr Brooks gulped and closed his eyes as every boy and girl in the school, as well as a few teachers, piled on. There was a muffled cry of 'don't hurt me!' as Mr Brooks disappeared under a mountain of bodies. Ajay blew his whistle sharply and waved his arms about a lot. Finally Mr Brooks emerged, looking dazed and confused.

'Orange card!' Ajay yelled at the head teacher.

'What did I do this time?' Mr Brooks said, spitting grass out of his mouth.

'Inciting violence and . . . er . . . offside.'

'Oh, this game is stupid!'

'Purple card for being rude to the game. Forfeit time.' Ajay smiled. 'You have to run around the outside of the field singing "I'm a silly sausage" for twenty minutes.'

Mr Brooks finally snapped. He broke the cricket bat over his knee and stormed off around the field.

'THIRTY MINUTES NOW!' Ajay yelled. 'There's an extra ten points deducted for being mean to a cricket bat.'

Violetta's home was on the other side of London, in a bleak part of the city. It was on the sort of street where no one goes after dark. Where it's cold and lonely, and the only sounds are people walking quickly away. This was where Violetta was happiest, a place where she could be alone with her grisly thoughts.

Violetta sat on a worn armchair in her lounge. The curtains were drawn and the only light came from the blue glow of the huge bank of TV screens fixed to the wall in front of her. Each one beamed news from around the world, and they all had Joe's face on them. He was now the most famous boy in the world. Violetta reached for a bottle on the side table and poured herself a large Scotch. The very sight of Joe made her skin scratchy with rage. Why wasn't *she* on every TV channel in the world? Why wasn't it *her* who everyone wanted to be seen with? Why, why, why? It was like a stuck record spinning around Violetta's head. She turned up the volume on one of the screens to drown out the questions whirring around in her brain.

'The new Prime Minister has been at it again—this time at his old school,' the news reporter was saying.

'He took time out from his busy schedule to bring laughter and silliness to the pupils of St Peter's, as well as inventing a new sport! In a couple of days, the park that Joe Perkins wanted to save is going to reopen, bigger and better than before.' Violetta pressed pause and rewound. '. . . silliness . . .' and again, '. . . silliness . . .' It was all too much for her to take, and she grabbed the first thing she laid her hands on and threw it at the bank of TVs on the wall, causing it to implode with a loud pop and shattering of glass.

'DRAT!' Violetta screamed, realizing she'd once again destroyed her phone. 'I can't take much more of this. I need a plan, I need to teach Perkins a lesson. I need to end this silliness now,' she muttered, fiddling with the brooch on her blouse. Suddenly her eyes lit up. She grabbed a pen and paper and began to scribble, frantically. 'I'm going to need a sharp pin, a fake dog poo, a set of screwdrivers, some wire cutters, banners, a few placards, and a legion of miserable people.' She laughed to herself. 'Ha ha, sometimes I scare myself! I'll give you a grand re-opening that you won't forget, Perkins!'

The final score was: Teachers 234 runs v Pupils 6-0 6-5 6-2. Man of the match, or rather woman of the match, went to Mrs Sanderson, who scored four conversions and took five wickets and tackled like a woman possessed. Jenkins, who had been watching the whole game from up the tree, clapped both teams politely.

'Excellent game, Prime Minister,' Jenkins said, as Joe and Ajay helped him down.

Just then, the sound of screeching tyres pierced the air and the Prime Ministerial car pulled up in a cloud of smoke.

'Prime Minister, I'm afraid you're needed,' Stevens said, winding down his window. 'I've come to escort you to the airport immediately!'

Jenkins turned his phone on and scrolled through a bank of messages urgently. His tone was serious. 'It's awful news. It looks as though the world may be on the brink of war. And you may be the only person who can stop it.'

WAR: WHAT IS IT GOOD FOR?

Joe held the phone to his ear.

'Hello . . . ?'

'Prime Meeenister?' a voice crackled from the other end.

'Yes . . . ?'

'I am ze Prezident of East Transilmania. And you have a lot to answer for.'

'I do?' said Joe, somewhat taken aback.

'Yes, we all saw you on zee news, with all your talk of zeeezing the day. Well the silly lot in

West Transilmania have done more than zeeeze the day, they've zeezed our land! You got us into this, now you can get us out, or it's war!' And with that the phone went dead.

'The government in East Transilmania is on the verge of war with West Transilmania and they're saying it's your fault!' Jenkins said, rubbing his hand through his hair as he read a news report from his phone. 'There's a set of mountains, well one mountain really, that they are both saying is theirs. It seems they were watching you on the news, talking about how one should live for the moment, and decided to take matters into their own hands. If they start a war with each other they'll only get everyone else involved and before you know it—World War Three!'

'Well, I guess you're right—I'll have to fix things and do whatever it takes to stop the war. I mean, I'm the Prime Minister—this is the kind of stuff I'm supposed to do, isn't it?' said Joe, uncertainly.

'Very well. We leave for West Transilmania right now.' Jenkins put his hands on Joe's shoulders and looked into his eyes. 'I believe in you, PM. The others will meet us at the airport.'

'Others . . . ?' Joe said.

'Well you didn't expect to go on holiday without taking your old mother, did you? Fourteen hours I was in labour with him and this is how he repays me!' Joe's mum was yelling at the top of her voice in front of a packed airport terminal. Joe's mum was always reminding him about how long it had taken him to be born.

Joe wasn't quite sure how he was supposed to respond to this. Should he apologize? Promise not to do it again? In the end he took to saying nothing and smiling.

'No, it's lovely to have you here, Mum. It was a surprise, that's all. And it's not a holiday, it's a summat.' Joe smiled, giving Jenkins a nod.

'SummIT,' Jenkins emphasized.

'Oh yes, one of those.'

Ajay, Joe, Jenkins, and Joe's mum walked through a special entrance at the side of the terminal and across the tarmac of the runway towards a small but smart-looking private jet.

'Hope you like your plane, sir?' Jenkins said as they climbed aboard. 'We added the modifications you requested.' It was an amazing sight. It had a real log-burning fire in it, for starters. A library. A ping-pong table, obviously. A big-screen TV, even more obviously. The normal plane seats had been replaced by sofas, and there was a pizza chef on board at all times too.

'Excellent work, Jenkins. If you're going to fly, fly in style, I say!' said Joe, looking around in awe.

'Well, quite!' Jenkins said. 'We shall arrive in comfort and refreshed.'

'Mum, are you doing anything tomorrow? You know, once we're back from the summit?' Joe asked.

'I thought I would dust down my park warden out-fit, ready for the grand opening tomorrow. If you manage to avert World War Three today, that is,' she replied.

'Well, I have a surprise for you. I'd really like you to be the guest of honour and cut the ribbon, at the park opening.'

'Oh darling, are you sure? I mean, me?' Joe's mum asked.

'Yeah, after all, you are the chief park warden. That place wouldn't be half as good if it wasn't for you!'

Joe's mum beamed. 'I can't believe it. You really are the best Prime Minister a mother could have.'

'Ha, my pleasure, Mum, my pleasure,' Joe chuckled.

'We're going to get our park back! I'm so happy I could do a somersault!' Ajay smiled.

'You totally should!'

Five hours later, they landed at West Transilmania airport. Everyone emerged from the plane slightly green and walking with a wobble. All except Ajay.

'I can't believe the captain let me fly the plane. What a guy! You should have seen his face when I did the first somersault. He was red with pride!'

Joe shook his head. He hadn't got the strength to talk, and feared that opening his mouth would result in instant projectile vomiting anyway. He was certain of one thing though. Ajay must never be allowed to control anything bigger than a remote-controlled car from now on. He was fairly sure he'd caught Jenkins sucking his thumb and praying at one point.

There was a car waiting for them on the runway. It was a big limousine that stretched out almost to the horizon, with flags on the front. They zipped through the streets like lightning before the limo pulled up outside a big, gothic-looking building.

'Ooh, how much do we owe you?' Mum shouted at the soundproof glass. 'HOW ... MUCH ... DO ... WE ... OWE ... YOU?'

'Mum, this isn't a taxi, we don't have to pay for it!' Joe told her. 'That's right, Jenkins, isn't it?'

'Yes, of course.'

Joe and his mini entourage got out of the car and walked up to the entrance, press from all over the world snapping cameras at them as they entered the summit building. It was a grand place, filled with marble walkways and huge, important-looking meeting rooms. Leaders from all over the world had joined the summit to do whatever they could to avert war.

'Jenkins,' Joe whispered. 'I'm nervous.'

'Sir, you're here for a reason. You are the Prime Minister. Think about what got you here—a desire to do the right thing. You're a good person. The world is waiting, Prime Minister,' Jenkins smiled.

'Thanks, Jenksy.' Joe took a deep breath, opened the door, and stepped into the summit room.

There were people everywhere and they all had ear pieces in. Joe was given his own and realized that it translated what anyone was saying into your own language. Either that, or it was to listen to the football scores.

138

'And now, let's hear from the British Prime Minister. See if he can sort this mess out,' said the President of East Transilmania, gesturing for Joe to step up to the podium.

The room fell silent and Joe could hear his own heartbeat thumping loudly in his ears. This was it— there was no going back now. The world was waiting. Joe cleared his throat and stepped up to the microphone.

'Good afternoon, the world. My name's Joe. The entire planet is watching us today. Speaking of which, I have a special mention for Ajay's nan in Mumbai: he says hi and he hopes the cream cleared your rash up.'

'That saved me five quid in phone charges.' Ajay winked at Jenkins from the back of the room.

'Where was I? Oh yes, the planet is watching and hoping that we can sort this out. So let's not let them down. War . . . hmmmm, let's be honest, war is rubbish, isn't it? I mean, yes we all love to dress up like soldiers and march around with medals on our chest when we're little, in fact I can see a few of you sat here who clearly still do. But there's more to war than dressing up and having a bit of a stomp and a

139

yell. There's all the killing for a start. And the cost. Paintballing is really expensive, so crikey knows how much war costs. Everyone always wants the latest gun, so the other countries won't laugh at you. All in all, war is pretty rubbish.' There were a few approving nods from the audience. 'All those in favour of war being "pretty rubbish" raise your hands?' Joe looked out across the crowd. 'One . . . two . . . three . . . yeah, just as I thought, loads, really loads. So the question is, what are we going to do about stopping another one?'

'They started it!'

Joe looked over to see who it was, and fortunately everyone had their name and country written on a badge at their desk. It was the President of East Transilmania.

The President of West Transilmania jumped up. 'No, they did. They stole our mountain! And we wouldn't be in this mess if it wasn't for you putting silly ideas into their heads,' the President said, pointing an accusing finger at Joe.

Everyone started shouting at each other and

within seconds half the room was caterwauling at the other half. It was total mayhem.

'IF YOU'LL EXCUSE ME, I HADN'T FINISHED!' Joe yelled, forcing the room to quieten down again. 'I didn't tell anyone to invade anywhere. All I wanted was for people to stop being so serious and have a bit of fun.'

'I was having fun. I find invading really good fun,' the President of East Transilmania explained.

'Invading isn't fun. Going down a twizzley slide so fast you feel like you need a wee is fun.

Popping bubble wrap is fun. Invading is bad and you know it!' Joe said, sternly. 'Let me get this straight. There's a mountain you both want, and you both think that it belongs to you? Am I right?'

'Yessss,' both men muttered.

'Well then, it's simple. Neither of you should have it.'

'WHAT?!' both presidents yelled at the same time.

'If you both can't play nicely, then neither of you should have the mountain. He can have it!' Joe cried, pointing randomly into the crowd of leaders. The King of Mongolia looked up, startled.

'I can have what?' he said, taking his earphones off.

'Weren't you listening?' Joe asked, a bit annoyed.

'Yes . . . but to the football scores.'

'What's the score?' the Italian Prime Minister asked.

'2–1 to Newcastle United.'

'It's so typical. My team always lose!' the Italian Prime Minister sighed, waving his arms about a bit.

'Do you know the baseball score too?' the American President joined in. The rest of the room sighed and tutted.

'Always with the baseball scores. Why don't you like football like everyone else? It makes me so sad,' the Italian Prime Minister said, shrugging his shoulders.

'Can we get back to business, please?' Joe bellowed. 'If you two can't agree whose mountain it is, then the simple solution is that neither of you have it and that guy gets to keep it.'

'But what if I don't want it?' the King of Mongolia said. 'To be honest, I already have quite a lot of mountains—I'm not sure where I'd put it.'

'Oh, don't worry, it's not a big mountain, more of a big hillock,' the President of East Transilmania replied.

'Yeah, it's pretty tiny really,' the President of West Transilmania agreed. 'We just call it the mountain because it's the only one we have.'

Joe rolled his eyes in frustration. 'We're not actually going to move the mountain, you great nincompoops, he just gets to say it's his. I dunno, he could perhaps name it, or stick a flag on it or something.'

'Jemima,' the King of Mongolia said, smiling.

'What?' Joe asked.

'I'd like to call it Jemima. The mountain, I mean.'

'I thought you didn't want it?' said Joe, feeling more confused by the second.

'Well, maybe I do now. Especially if I can call it Jemima.'

'I don't like Jemima,' said the President of East Transilmania.

'No, nor me. Can't we just keep the name it has now?' said the President of West Transilmania.

'Well, what's it called now?' Joe asked impatiently.

'Mount Lovely,' both Presidents replied.

'Awww,' the whole of the room cooed.

'Yeah, it is lovely,' said the President of East Transilmania.

'Well, I don't know,' said Joe, 'I mean it could be called Mount Lovely if you like, but that would mean learning to share. Can you learn to share it?' Joe asked earnestly.

The President of West Transilmania consulted with his advisor.

'We could have it Mondays, Wednesdays and Fridays, and you could have it Tuesdays, Thursdays and Saturdays?'

'Hmmm . . .' the other President consulted with his team. 'I can't do Tuesdays, I have zumba that night. Could we swap Tuesdays for Mondays?'

'Yeah, OK.'

'What about Sundays?'

'Sundays I could have it and call it Jemima! Oh, go ooooon!' the King of Mongolia pleaded.

The presidents of East and West Transilmania whispered something to each other.

'All right, but promise you'll take care of it,' the West Transilmanian President offered.

'Yeah, it is lovely after all!' the President of East Transilmania chipped in.

'Of course. Why don't you two come for a picnic on it or something on Sunday? We can have sandwiches and a game of frisbee.'

'OK!'

'You see, that wasn't so hard now, was it? War avoided. Picnic arranged. We've called a mountain Jemima one day a week,' Joe smiled, checking his watch, 'and I reckon we can still make the second half of the football!'

The room burst into applause. Joe had done it, he had actually done it! Jenkins looked utterly speechless for once and Ajay ran over and gave Joe a hug. It was nice but a bit awkward. Joe had never been hugged by Ajay before. Mum came over and gave him a kiss and squeeze, which was even more embarrassing in front of his new friends.

'Well done, son. I knew you could do it. Excellent use of the "if you can't play nicely, then you don't play at all" tactic!' Mum smiled.

'Well I learnt from the master.'

Jenkins walked over, a look of shock still on his face.

'I know what you're going to say—that was a stupid thing to do. To be so risky . . . but it was . . .'

'Brilliant!' Jenkins said, laughing.

'OK, I didn't know what you were going to say.'

'It was pure brilliance, Prime Minister. You did it. You actually did it,' and for the first time since Joe had come to office, a huge grin beamed across Jenkins' face. It was the first time Joe felt as though he'd done some good in the world. Yeah, he'd made people smile, but this was important: he'd actually stopped a war!

PARKLIFE

It was a gloriously sunny day and Joe was feeling pretty good about life. Yesterday, he'd stopped a war, today he was going to reopen his beloved park. By midday a huge crowd had gathered by the gates, all waiting for the grand opening. There was a carnival atmosphere—adults and kids getting their faces painted, fairground rides, and a band. Joe and Ajay arrived by jet pack just as Jenkins and Joe's mum pulled up in the limo. Joe undid his pack and gazed through the gates. It was such a huge change from the last time they were there. The bulldozers had gone, the grass had been fixed and the playground rebuilt, bigger and better. There was a huge bouncy castle, a massive sandpit, and giant curly slides.

'You did it, Joe.' Ajay smiled. 'You actually did it.'

'We did it,' Joe said, looking at all the happy faces everywhere. Well, almost everywhere. At the back of the park, in the shadow of a big oak tree, was a woman dressed in black from head to toe, with a single broach pinned to her top, glinting in the sunshine. She was wearing a hoodie with the hood pulled down low and had a black rucksack on her back. When no one was looking, she slinked round to the park fence and pulled a pair of wire cutters from her bag. She gave one last look around as she snipped into the fence, before scurrying back into the trees. Next, she pulled out a fake dog poo and a spanner from her top pocket.

'Let's see how well your grand opening goes after I get busy with this lot, Perkins,' Violetta hissed.

'Mum, it's time!' Joe said, excitedly. 'Ajay, do you have the over-sized comedy scissors?'

'Right here, boss.'

Joe walked over to the microphone, flanked by Ajay and his mum.

'Today is a very special day because not only have we got our park back, but my mum has her job back too. I used to play here all the time when I was a kid. I mean, I still am a kid, but when I was even smaller, this place meant the world to me. Ajay and me would spend hours here, kicking a ball around or playing hide and seek.'

'A hundred and fifty games undefeated!' Ajay yelled, before doing a fist-pump. 'Oops, sorry.'

Joe smiled. 'Anyway, as you know, all I ever wanted to do was save this place, so kids like me could enjoy it. Parks shouldn't be knocked down to build flats on. We want more parks, not fewer. And so it gives me a great pleasure to ask my mum, the park's Chiefiest of all Wardens, to do the honour of cutting the ribbon.'

Joe's mum's face was a giddy mixture of happiness and self-consciousness. She gave Joe a kiss and ruffled his hair.

'Muuuuum!' Joe whined with slight embarrassment.

'I now declare the new park open, gawd bless her and all that sail in her.'

'That's ships, Mum,' Joe whispered.

'Ooops, oh well. Just have a good time everyone.

Grand Re-opening

Now I reckon we should let our new Prime Minister be the first one to try the bouncy castle.'

'Oh, I don't know . . . !'

'Go on, Prime Minister,' came a voice from the crowd. Joe turned around. There was something familiar about that voice. But then the rest of the crowd joined in, and Joe forgot all about it.

'Oh, OK!' Joe ran over to the giant bouncy castle and hopped on board. He began to bounce and couldn't help letting out a few 'wheeeeeees' as he leapt higher and higher. 'Come on, everyone. Let's all see how high we can go!' Within moments the whole place was jumping. Literally.

'Perfect timing, PM,' Violetta cackled. She pulled the brooch out and looked at the light shimmering off the pin, before stabbing it into the back of the bouncy castle.

KAAAAAAAA-BOOOOOOOOOOOOOM!

There were pieces of bouncy castle flying through the air in every direction, landing on people's faces like a hot rubbery custard pie. Everyone—boys, girls, and grown-ups—were flung in every direction when the bouncy castle exploded. One old lady landed by the ice-cream van, knocking the entire queue over like a set of fleshy dominos. Violetta hurried over to the sandpit and flung the fake poo in like a grenade.

'Eeeeew!' one toddler screamed. 'Someone's done ploppy in the sand!'

'That's disgusting!' a parent shouted. 'Did your child do that? You should be ashamed. This is why I hate fun!'

'How dare you! My son didn't do that. Perhaps it was yours!' A huge row erupted in the sandpit, with mums and dads screaming at each other, throwing sand in great big fistfuls.

'What's happening?' Ajay yelled.

'I don't know!' Joe's mum replied. 'Help! I can't get out of this bouncy castle!'

In the chaos, Violetta crawled on hands and knees to the candy floss machine and unscrewed a pipe. Within seconds, the machine was spinning out of control, flinging candy floss in every direction. A bald man got it all over his head. He looked like he was wearing a sticky pink wig.

Joe had been flung from the bouncy castle when it exploded and was now wedged between the balloon stand, and the stall where you won a giant teddy if you hooked a tiny duck on a stick the size of a pole vault. He watched open-mouthed as his dream of saving the park turned into a nightmare. He felt helpless. There was a fight in the sandpit, the bouncy castle had blown up, and people were running around in a panic, covered from head to toe in candy floss. And to make matters worse, there were gaping holes in the fence. Those jagged edges were a health and safety nightmare!

'None of this would have happened if the Prime Minister hadn't jumped so high,' one man yelled.

'Yeah, he was having too much fun and now look what's happened. He's ruined it!' a mother yelled.

'This is why I don't like joviality, it always goes wrong!' someone else joined in.

153

'But . . . but I wasn't jumping too high. I mean, I didn't mean to. I was just having a laugh,' Joe called, trying to free himself and knocking over the coconut shy in the process.

'A laugh?!' The man with candy floss on his head yelled. 'Do I look funny to you?'

'No . . . well . . . a little. I mean, I'm sorry. I just want people to enjoy themselves!' Joe tried to explain.

'You want to enjoy yourself, but what about the rest of us?' a woman shrieked.

'One rule for us, one rule for them,' another person said. 'I thought he was different.'

'But . . . but . . . !' Joe started.

'Oh, Prime Minister?' the woman in black yelled. 'Smile please, for your number one fan!'

Joe automatically turned round and gave the best grin he could muster. 'I'm sorry, I don't have time for any more pictures—I need to sort this mess out!'

'I think it's time to leave,' Jenkins said, helping Joe to his feet. 'You better let your mother and me deal with this. There are too many press people here, and we don't want your picture all over the papers.'

Violetta slipped her camera back into her bag and ran through the trees towards the fence. She squeezed her bony body through the gap and out into the streets. Pulling down her hood, she grabbed her phone from her bag and began to dial.

'Hi, it's me. I have a picture you might be interested in. The Prime Minister grinning like a fool in the middle of a disaster he is responsible for . . .'

PANIC ON THE
STREETS OF LONDON

Joe was sitting up in bed, in his Postman Pat pyjamas, surrounded by the morning's newspapers.

'Have you seen the news . . . ?' Jenkins asked, poking his head round the door. 'Ah, you have.'

'"Park-a-geddon!", "PM Left Deflated!", "Joe So Low After Big Park Blow Show!", "Elvis Found on Moon" . . . these headlines are just awful, and they all have a picture of me smiling with my thumbs up. ALL OF THEM! Someone asked me for my picture, they said "smile"! I thought that was the right thing to do.'

'I know, sir. It seems as though it was taken by some-one at the opening. They must have sold it to the papers. Ajay's downstairs and he wants to know if you're all right.'

Joe got out of bed mournfully and slid down the fireman's pole he'd had installed from his bedroom to the corridor below.

'Whoah! Joe, you look seriously down. Are you going to get dressed or wear those Postman Pat PJs all day?' Ajay asked, looking concerned.

'Maybe if I'd taken this job more seriously, it wouldn't have come to this.'

'Wait a minute, Joe. Having fun doesn't make bouncy castles explode, right?'

An office door off the corridor opened and a woman slid out on an office chair. 'Most bouncy castle accidents are due to a sudden loss of pressure, from a pin prick for example With that, the worker disappeared again.

'See!' Ajay said. 'It wasn't your fault.'

'Well, well, well. There's a terrible sight.' Violetta came stalking down the corridor towards Joe, looking happier than Joe had ever seen her. 'How was the opening?'

'Oh leave me alone, you know exactly how it went—you must have seen the papers. Don't you worry, I'll rebuild the park bigger and better next time!' Joe surprised himself by shouting at Violetta.

'Well if it isn't our Prime Minister being all grumpy. Where's the laughter and smiles gone, Joe? Finding it a bit tough, are we? This is worth a picture.' Violetta pulled out her phone and was about to click the button.

'Leave me alone,' Joe snapped and turned to walk away.

'Oh go on, smile please, it's for your number one fan . . .' Violetta laughed.

Joe stopped still. 'It was you! You took that picture of me and sent it to the papers!'

'Well done, blancmange brain,' Violetta said nonchalantly. 'It was such a good picture I couldn't resist sending it to all the papers.'

'But it makes me look bad, like I was laughing at other people's misfortune. I wasn't doing that, you know I wasn't!'

'Save the excuses, a picture paints a thousand words, remember!' Violetta said, holding the photo of

Joe right up to his face. 'The park's closed now, and it's going to stay closed. I don't think it'll ever open again after what happened. Your mother must be so proud!'

'You're... YOU'RE...!' Joe screamed.

'I'M WHAT?!'

'YOU'RE FIIIIIIIIRED!'

Violetta stared at Joe and slowly a smile spread across her face. 'Thank you,' she said, and walked off chuckling to herself.

'What...?' Joe was confused. 'Jenkins, what did she mean by 'thank you'?'

'I don't know, sir. I just don't know.'

Joe spent the rest of the morning in a daze, replaying everything over and over in his head. He had just wanted to do the right thing by his mum, and now look what had happened. And what had Violetta meant when she'd said thank you?

Joe was supposed to be signing a new law to make sweets one of your five-a-day, but he just couldn't concentrate. He looked up, startled, as Jenkins burst in, switching the TV on and grabbing the remote.

'Sir, you need to see this,' he said urgently.

'You join us here in central London for some huge news. Violetta Crump, the deputy Prime Minister, has been fired. She is about to make a statement.' The camera cut to Violetta, standing in front of Number Ten.

'The Prime Minister—if such a grand word can be used for such a small child—took it upon himself to force enjoyment on everyone in this country. I begged him not to force everyone to have fun, but instead of listening to me, he fired me. That's the kind of Prime Minister we have. One who only thinks about himself, and no one else. Yesterday, we saw the awful consequences of that decision. Yesterday, we saw the true cost of fun—misery for men, women, and children. People need order in their life, they need rules. They need to be told what to do! What we don't need is a four-foot clown in charge.'

'Hey, I'm four foot six!' Joe yelled at the TV.

'Ask yourself what kind of country you want. One where a boy—that's right, a boy—tells you what to do? We're a joke. We've all seen the YouTube clips of bouncy castles bursting, people getting stuck in slides. Children hurt by flying hot dogs. We don't have a leader, we have an entertainer. What next? What if the world is on the brink of another crisis? Is Joe going to make some balloon animals, try a spot of juggling? Well I for one am not laughing. And neither is Mr Johnson.'

A middle-aged man moved towards the microphone, looking miserable and cross.

'Mr Johnson is a taxi driver. An ordinary member of the public, forced to dress up in fancy dress by our Prime Minister for his entertainment. Mr Johnson, if you would like to tell the public how it is.'

'I was just trying to earn a living, until Joe Perkins came long. Suddenly that's not enough, now I'm being told to dress up just to keep my customers entertained. Well, it turns out I'm allergic to synthetic fibres, the sort that you get in fancy dress costumes, and I was off work for a week. I mean you should see the rash on my . . .'

'Thank you, Mr Johnson,' Violetta grabbed the microphone back.

'It's all up one side of my bottom. Bright red like a huge radish.' Mr Jonson leant in to the microphone to finish what he was saying.

'We don't need to put you through any more indignity,' Violetta shouted over him.

'Dignity? That went a long time ago. What won't go is the bleedin' rash. I mean, who knew a tutu could do that to a man's behind? I can show you if you like?'

To everyone's horror the taxi driver began to undo his trousers.

'NO!' Violetta yelled, before wrestling Mr Johnson off screen.

'Also meet Mrs Grey,' Violetta said, returning and beckoning a lady forward from the crowd. 'Mrs Grey had a terrible experience, isn't that right, dear?'

'I read in the papers that cats should have to wear hats, so I decided that little Billy should wear a top hat, and now I can't get it off.' Mrs Grey pulled her cat from a box next to her to show to the world. 'I had to make little holes at the front so he can see where he's going and another hole so I can feed him his din-dins. He looks ridiculous. None of the other cats will talk to him.'

'I didn't make that woman force a hat on her cat!' Joe shouted at the TV. 'Why are they blaming me, Jenkins?' Joe turned to look at his chief advisor. 'Well? I thought you had all the answers?'

'There are hundreds of these stories up and down the country, about people being forced to join in and have fun,' continued Violetta. 'Well, no more I say! No more of being told that being silly is the new normal. That's why today I'm resigning from the government. I can't be a part of this nonsense anymore. I'm announcing the formation of a new organization—one that's going to hold you to account, Prime Minister. Today I'm announcing the birth of the Anti-Silliness League!'

Joe watched in amazement as Violetta was joined

on the platform by angry-looking men and women of all ages. They were the type of people who tell you not to play ball on the grass. The type of people who tell you to be quiet if you're laughing too loudly. People who sit behind twitching net curtains. The sort who tut so everyone can hear them and roll their eyes a lot. The sort for whom Christmas is an inconvenience. The kind who sneer when it's someone's birthday. Who pop balloons just for the heck of it. The type who walk on little kids' sandcastles. Joe felt a shiver ripple down his back. He'd only been watching for a few seconds, yet instantly he knew everything he needed to know about this horde of misery guts.

'This country used to be great! We used to be a nation people admired, but now look at us, we're a laughing stock. And only one person is to blame for this and that's Joseph Perkins! Down with Perkins!' Violetta chanted.

Soon her little gang of followers were all chanting with her. 'DOWN WITH PERKINS! DOWN WITH PERKINS! DOWN WITH PERKINS! DOWN WITH PERKINS!'

'Joe Perkins, I challenge you to a serious live TV debate. Just you and me. Let's see who the people really want as their leader now!' Violetta shoved her face right in the camera, so she filled the whole screen. It felt as though she was looking right at Joe. 'Come on, Perkins. For once, why don't you show some guts!'

Joe switched the TV off—he couldn't take any more.

'Sir, you're not going to do it, are you? You're not going to rise to her bait?' Jenkins asked.

'If I don't, people will say I'm a coward,' Joe replied miserably.

'You don't have to do anything you don't want to.' Ajay shrugged.

'If I don't then she'll win. Her and her miserable mob. I have to meet her and have it out with her once and for all.'

Joe got up and made his way to the door.

'I just need to get out of these PJs. You were right, Ajay, they are stupid.'

'Hey, I never said that . . .' Ajay called after Joe, but it was too late. He was already gone.

It was dusk by the time Joe arrived at the TV studios. He'd put on his smartest suit, combed his hair, and slicked it down with gel. He looked at himself in the mirror. 'If she wants serious, I'll give her serious,' Joe muttered.

Ajay came into Joe's dressing room. 'Hey, you're properly going through with this then? Don't we need to talk about this? I am your media manager and friend forward slash lifestyle guru, you know, mate!'

'This is something I need to do on my own,' Joe sighed.

'Well, fair enough, good luck, then,' said Ajay, reaching out to shake Joe's hand.

'Thanks mate . . . WHAAAAAAAA!' Joe snatched his hand back from a sudden electric shock.

'Ha ha ha ha! You can't beat a hand buzzer. Here, you can have it. I thought you could use it on Violetta.'

'This is serious!' Joe snapped.

'Oh come on, you used to love the buzzer!' said Ajay, laughing.

'Don't laugh at me,' Joe yelled. 'I have to show

her who's in charge and play her at her own game. I can't have my authority undermined.'

'Your what undermined? Wow, now you sound like a politician!'

'In case you hadn't noticed, Ajay, that is what I am,' Joe said sarcastically.

'Look at yourself,' said Ajay, shaking his head. 'I've never seen you in a suit before. You look weird. This isn't the Joe that I helped become Prime Minister.'

'Weird, huh?! I wasn't so weird when you wanted to come over for sleep-overs, or scoff jelly in the cabinet room,' Joe shouted.

'What's that supposed to mean?' Ajay said, going red in the face.

'If it wasn't for me . . . then no one would even CARE who you were!'

'If it wasn't for me, *you* wouldn't be Prime Minister.'

'You didn't do this, it was me! I'm the one they wanted for once, NOT YOU!' Joe stopped short and put his hand over his mouth but he was too angry to apologize.

Ajay just shook his head. He didn't look angry, just hurt.

A young woman with a clipboard and headphones poked her head round the corner of the dressing room. 'You're on in one minute Prime Mini—everything OK?'

'I was just leaving,' Ajay said, walking away.

'Everything's fine, in fact everything's much better now,' Joe said, so Ajay could hear.

'Well you'd better get ready to go on,' said the woman, shoving Joe towards the stage.

It was the first time Joe had been in a TV studio, and it felt big and imposing. The crowd had also been whipped up into a frenzy. It felt more like a boxing match than a debate. In one corner stood Joe, the Prime Minister, but also just a kid. In the other was Violetta, the one person who was out to destroy him. Should he come out fighting, or should he be nice and try to reason with her? He wished Jenkins was here, or his mum, but they weren't. For the first time ever, Joe felt truly alone.

Someone with earphones and a clipboard pushed him through the gap and onto the stage. Joe's legs felt heavy—like he wasn't going to be able to make it to the middle without falling over. In the centre of the stage were two chairs—one for him, one for Violetta. She strode out confidently from the other side of the stage, towards him. They met in the middle. Joe held out his hand for her to shake. She smiled and took it, shaking it with a vice-like grip.

'I'm going to crush you,' she whispered with a fixed smile on her face.

Joe tried to be brave, but he was petrified! He could have done with the handshake buzzer right about now.

Lastly the presenter made his entrance. 'Laaaaaaadies and gentlemen! Welcome to this special debate. Violetta Crump versus the Prime Minister of Great Britain in one of the most anticipated battles in history. It's Tom-foolery versus the Anti-Silliness League. It's kids against grown-ups! There can be only one winner! You decide! Violetta, Prime Minister, let the show begin!'

Joe looked out at the audience. They were dressed in ninety per cent beige. This wasn't a fair fight—this was an Anti-Silliness League rally! It was a trap and he'd walked right into it.

There was no time to think. The bright lights suddenly dimmed and the audience hushed to an excitable silence.

'Thank you, Prime Minister, for coming here tonight. It's very brave of you,' Violetta said. She had a look on her face as though she was about to stamp on a cockroach that had been bugging her all day.

'My pleasure, Ms Crump. Always nice to see you,' Joe said, trying to smile.

'Do you want to start the debate now, or do you

have a few impressions to do first? Perhaps tell some jokes, maybe throw a custard pie or two?' Violetta said, raising an eyebrow. 'We all know how much you like a laugh.'

'No,' said Joe. Whatever tiny grin he had on his face fell away. 'I don't think this lot would find it very funny somehow.'

'Too clever for them, are you?' Violetta said, pretending to be shocked. There was a sharp intake of breath from the audience.

'What I mean is . . .' Joe tried correcting himself.

'I think we all know what you mean, Prime Minister. I think the country is beginning to see what kind of a person you really are. Certainly we in the Anti-Silliness League know what sort of person you are. Laughing at other people's misfortune. You think you're better than us? I haven't even heard you say sorry for the park debacle yet. Someone could have been hurt.'

'I am sorry, but, I mean, what happened at the park . . . it was an accident.'

'Quite a few accidents happen to you. You *accidentally* became the Prime Minister, you

173

accidentally almost started a war, you *accidentally* burst a bouncy castle. How long before someone *accidentally* gets killed!'

'That's not fair! Perhaps there was a problem with the equipment at the park,' Joe started.

'Blaming someone else I see, Prime Minister,' Violetta hissed. 'How childish.' The crowd let out a few ironic laughs.

'No . . .'

'You think by appearing on YouTube for a few minutes, it somehow makes you important?' Violetta interrupted.

There were a few boos from the crowd and someone shouted, 'You tell him, Violetta!'

'Well . . . yes, I mean no . . .' Joe tried to explain, but he just couldn't get the words right.

'Oh I see,' Violetta continued. 'You think you're better than everyone. It's OK for you to do it, but it's not right for anyone else.'

'No!' Joe shouted. 'No. I think we're all the same, we need to look after each other and try to have some fun. All I want to do is—'

'Oh, here it comes. Now you're going to tell me what to do, what to think, how to behave?' Violetta hissed. 'Isn't it time to put the grown-ups back in charge? We've seen what happens when we let the children play. Accident after accident. Is this what the country needs?'

'I tried my best. It wasn't my fault, I didn't do it on purpose.' Joe felt helpless.

'What wasn't your fault? The bouncy castle exploding, you being Prime Minister? Tell us Joe, what happened?'

'It was a mistake!' Joe yelled.

'The whole thing's been a mistake.'

'I'll say it was a mistake. Having you as Prime Minister. You're the real joke, Perkins.'

The crowd were beside themselves, booing and hissing at Joe so he couldn't think. Violetta was right, what was he doing? He was just a boy—what made him think he could run a country? Joe slowly unplugged the mic from his shirt, and dropped it. The crowd jeered him off stage like a pantomime villain.

It was dark by the time Joe got back to Downing Street, and his skin was itchy and restless with exhaustion. The TV debate had finished hours ago, but Joe asked Stevens to drive him round town for a while.

'Thanks, Stevens,' Joe said as he got out of the car.

'Keep your pecker up, PM. I know things seem bad now, but you wait, things will sort themselves out.'

'Bad?' Joe managed a laugh. 'I dream of when things improve to get as good as "bad".'

Joe wearily walked to the front door and pushed it open. Jenkins stood by the stairs, his tie undone. He looked as exhausted as Joe.

'Does Sir need anything?' he asked.

'No,' Joe said. 'Did you watch the debate?'

'Yes I did.' Jenkins sighed. 'You played right into her hands.'

'Can we save it until tomorrow, Jenkins? I'm really not in the mood.'

'If you carry on like this, there won't be many more tomorrows,' said Jenkins, as Joe just shrugged his shoulders and made his way up the stairs to bed.

Jenkins watched him go and then the phone in his pocket began to ring. Who would be calling this late? He reached for his phone, looked at the screen, and then answered.

'I've been expecting you to ring. I'm surprised it's taken this long.'

'You know me, I'm full of surprises.'

'You don't have to tell me, Violetta.'

'I think it's about time we had a little chat . . .'

15

THAT JOKE ISN'T FUNNY ANYMORE

'Good evening and welcome to a special report. I'm Charlie James. It's only been in existence for a few weeks, but already the Anti-Silliness League is having a huge effect. We see them every day, wearing their Anti-Silliness League badges with pride. Is this a real political movement or a flash in the pan? We spoke to one clown, who asked us to keep his identity a secret.

'Tell me what the last few days have been like for you.'

'A nightmare. I mean, it's no laughing matter. I have to go everywhere in disguise so people don't know I'm a clown,' said the shadowy figure, his silhouette revealing the round nose and curly wig that are the stock in trade of clowns.

'I know a few other clowns who have been forced to give up because of this Anti-Silliness stuff. You know, because of the stigma of it all. It all started going wrong when we got sued for throwing a custard pie in someone's face. And soon after that, protesters turned up and started yelling abuse at me and the other clowns. No one needs to take that, do they? We were forced underground . . . Secret clowning around. Every so often we put on our big shoes again and perform in disused car parks or abandoned warehouses. It's not the same, but you know, it's better than nothing,' the clown said with a sigh.

'And that's not all,' Charlie continued. 'We hear that joke shops are closing down all the time. It's getting harder and harder to buy rubber chickens or stink bombs anywhere. And the one big question tonight is, where is the Prime Minister? Has he given up on the country? Have we seen the last of Joe Perkins?'

'I want more jelly. Someone get me jelly. Lime-flavoured. I want lime.' Joe sat in the Prime Ministerial jelly room in his pants, shoving great gloppy spoonfuls of jelly into his face.

'HE-LLO. I SAID JELLY! WHERE IS EVERYONE?'

Joe yelled, spraying jelly everywhere.

Jenkins walked in carrying a bowl of jelly with a sombre look on his face.

'About time, Jenkins.'

'I think Sir may have had enough jelly for one day,' Jenkins said, making an attempt to clear the room.

'Nonsense! I've only had seven bowls this morning.'

'I think seven is plenty. Besides which, you have a visitor,' Jenkins said, mopping the jelly globs from the wall. 'I'll leave you two to it—I have to make a phone call.'

'Coooooeeee, son.' Mum was hovering in the doorway, looking worriedly at Joe.

'Oh no . . .' Joe sighed, putting his bowl and spoon down.

'How are you, Joe?' Mum asked, struggling to smile.

'FINE!' Joe spluttered. Hard to do with a mouth full of jelly.

'I saw Ajay yesterday. He's still pretty upset about your argument, you know.'

Joe swallowed the last of the jelly.

'He is angry, but he'll get over that. I think mostly he's worried. We all are. And it's not like you two to argue.'

'Well, people change,' Joe said grumpily.

'Ajay didn't seem like he'd changed. Except maybe he looked a bit sadder.'

'Oh I see, so you're saying I *have* changed? Is that right?' Joe tossed his dish to one side and folded his arms crossly.

'Joe, you're sitting in your pants eating jelly. I think it's fair to say this is a new level of weird.'

Mum pulled Joe up by the hand and hoisted him over to the window. 'Joe, what do you see?'

'What?'

'Just say what you see.'

'A mother who's assaulting her son?'

'Stop it. Tell me what you see!'

'All right, all right. I see London, people, policemen, buildings, a seagull doing its business . . .'

'I see a country who needs a leader!' Mum yelled triumphantly. 'There's people out there who need you, Joe, people who believed in you. Isn't it about time you believed in you too?'

'They don't need me. They don't want me. People are too afraid to joke on the streets anymore, not because of this silly Anti-Silliness League, but because of me! I'm Prime Minister and I couldn't even manage to save one blooming park,' Joe yelled, tears stinging in his eyes. 'Everything is a mess and it's all my fault! It's all my fault.'

'Oh, Joe. There'll be other parks, but I only have one son. We have to concentrate on saving you first. I can get another job somewhere else,' she said, giving him a big cuddle.

In a run-down park not far from Downing Street, Jenkins was wearing a pair of large, dark sun-glasses and taking a seat on a park bench. He checked his pocket watch and looked around.

'PSSSST!'

PSSST!

The noise was coming from the bushes behind him. Jenkins turned around and peered over his glasses.

'Could you be any more obvious, Violetta?' Jenkins tutted.

'You can talk. Nice sunglasses—did they come free in a cracker? I thought you weren't coming,' she said, standing up and brushing the leaves off her head.

'You can't be too careful. I didn't want anyone to see me . . .'

'Talking to the likes of me? This is what power is all about,' she exclaimed. 'The TV stuff, the things we do in front of the camera, that's just a show, a circus act for the fools at home. This is where the real stuff happens—whispered conversations in secret. The question is—why are *you* here? I mean, it's obvious what I want, I want Perkins' job. But what is it you want, Jenkins? You're certainly not here because you like me, are you?'

'I'm . . . I'm a realist. That means I like to keep my options open. I've been in this job long enough to know when a Prime Minister is finished. I know the way the wind is blowing and I know it's only a matter of time before Perkins has to go. I also know that bouncy castles just don't explode by themselves,' Jenkins said lifting up his glasses.

'I thought I made the whole thing quite convincing.'

'I knew it was you,' Jenkins nodded.

'Closing one park is just the start of it! Once I've finished Joe off, the Anti-Silliness League will sweep to power. No more parks anywhere! Roller-coasters, trampolines, curly slides, pirate ships, all gone for ever! Who needs fun when you can make money?!' Violetta cleared her throat and sat down next to Jenkins. 'Being PM will give me the chance to make school lessons twice as long. That way, by the time they all leave at twelve years old they'll be ready to work for a living. No more of that loathsome enjoyment, just hard, honest work. Laughter is for the weak. Fun is for imbeciles. We'll be the richest nation on earth! But like I said—what do you want, Jenkins?'

'I want my country back. There's a child in charge of the country that I love and I can't take any more.' Jenkins undid his coat to reveal an Anti-Silliness League badge on the inside lapel.

Violetta grinned with delight. 'You can be my deputy and have it all. Money, houses, whatever you want. All you have to do is persuade that horrible little oik to resign, and hand over power to me. He'll listen to you. You just wait until the time is right and then convince the little twerp. Then it can be all yours.'

'How will I know when it's the right time?' Jenkins asked.

'Oh, you'll know. Just think of it. You and me working together. We can have whatever we want. You never know, Jenkins, you might even grow to like me. What do you say?'

Jenkins looked at Violetta and smiled.

16

ALL BY MYSELF

The sun was shining through the curtains but Joe was still in bed, staring at the ceiling. It had all seemed so easy a few weeks ago but now things were a mess. Joe slipped on a coat over his pyjamas, added a massive hat as a disguise, and headed outside.

There was no one about. Probably because the Anti-Silliness League seemed to be everywhere—stopping fun at every turn. Joe kept his head down and walked aimlessly. When he looked up, he was outside the park gates. It had been closed since that fateful day. Joe gazed through the gates, looking at what remained of his brilliant park. What hadn't had been chained up had been dismantled. An Anti-Silliness League poster tied to the gates flapped about in the cool morning breeze.

Joe looked at it and sighed. He didn't even have enough energy to tear it down. He kept walking—all he wanted to do was escape the sadness inside, but it just wouldn't leave him alone. Goodness knows how long he'd been walking, but something snapped him out of his daze. Right across the road there was a factory. Joe had seen it hundreds of times before, but he'd never really paid much attention to it. Today, though, it was different. There was something familiar about the shadow in the window. Joe walked up to the security guard at the gates.

'Excuse me. What does this factory make?' Joe asked.

'Do I know you?' the man said, trying to get a glimpse of Joe under his massive hat.

'I live round here,' Joe said, trying to disguise his voice. 'That's probably where you've seen me before.'

'Oh, right. Well, you know pork pies?'

'Er . . . yeah . . .'

'You know the jelly that you get in them?'

'Yeah . . .'

'Well, this is the place that puts the jelly into pork pies,' he said, shrugging his shoulders. 'I know, pretty grim, huh? I wouldn't like to be stuck inside for twelve hours a day, pumping a pie full of goop. Nope, not me.'

Joe peered at the shadowy figure in the window, trying to see if it was . . . yes—it was! It was his mum. He'd know that bouffant hair anywhere. His mum

was working in a pork pie factory! She hated those things. It was too much for Joe to take, and he turned and ran.

'You all right, son?' the security man called after him.

Joe's feet pounded the streets. Not only had he failed to save the park, but now his mum was working in the one place that she probably hated the most.

'Arrrrrgh!' Joe yelled, coming to an abrupt halt after suddenly being soaked to the skin by cold water. 'What on earth?'

'Oops! Sorry, I thought you were Zook from the planet Neptune.'

Joe shivered and turned to see a girl of about eight sitting on a tricycle in her front garden. She was clutching a super-soaker.

'What are you talking about?!' Joe said, wiping the water from his face.

'Zook. Oh come on, you must have heard of him? Squelching aliens is such fun.'

'No! And I think it's very silly to go around firing water pistols at people. You should stop it right away.

Don't be so childish!'

'Oh, you're one of those aunties,' she said knowingly.

'One of what?'

'An Aunty Silliness person. I've heard about them on the TV.'

'The Anti-Silliness League, I think you mean,' Joe snapped.

'That's what I said. They're even more dangerous than Zook from the planet Neptune.' And with that she squirted him again.

'Oi!' Joe bellowed. 'Stop doing that! And no, I'm not one of those people. I'M THE PRIME MINISTER!'

'What's a Prime Minister?' the girl said, confused.

'It means I'm in charge.'

'I hate Prime Ministers.'

'How can you hate them when you don't even know what one is?'

'All they do is go around shouting at people and tell them what to do and ruining everyone's fun.'

'I don't do that!'

'You just did!'

Joe didn't know what to say. He had just told her off when all she wanted to do was have fun. Joe took off his massive hat and scratched his head.

'What's your name?'

'Suzi. And the way I see it is that you can't beat giggles. Take the other day, for example: I did the squeakiest, longest fart ever. I timed it at 35.3 seconds.'

'That's gross. And you time them?!'

'Duh, yeah, how else are you supposed to write them down on the fart chart? Anyway, the thing is, it made me laugh so much that I fell over. I fall over a lot.'

'So do I actually,' Joe said, smiling in spite of himself.

'Great isn't it? One moment you're walking along, the next you're flying through the air. Falling is the best.'

'I get embarrassed. In case someone laughs,' Joe said, looking down shyly.

'Who cares? It's good to laugh at yourself. Sometimes I stand in front of the mirror pulling funny faces to make myself laugh. I can spend a whole afternoon doing it.'

Suzi pulled some daft faces that made Joe laugh. It was a small, almost apologetic laugh at first.

'I like to have croaking competitions too. Want to see who can croak like a frog the longest?

CROOOOOOOOOOOOOOOO OOOOOOOAAAAAAAAA AAAKKKKKKKKKKKK...'

Suzi began.

Joe looked around nervously in case anyone was watching. But so what if they were? Croaking in the street wouldn't have bothered him a few weeks ago. He took a deep breath.

'CROOOOOOOOOOOOOOOOOO OOOOOOOOOOOAAAAAAAAA AAAAAKKKKKKKKKKKKKKKK KKKKKKKKKKKKKKKK...'

Joe couldn't keep it in any longer. He started to laugh. Properly this time. 'You win!'

'Yes!'

'You don't have another one of those super-soakers by any chance?'

'I have a whole stash. Why?'

'Because I think Zook is coming,' Joe said, pointing at the postman. 'And as Prime Minister it is my job to protect the planet!'

'Welcome aboard, PM!' Suzi yelled.

ROCKET MAN

Joe burst through the doors at Downing Street and threw off his soggy coat and massive hat. He was finally starting to feel like his old self again, and it felt good.

'JENKINS,

I NEED JENKINS!'

Joe yelled in his biggest, boomiest voice.

'What is it, sir?' Jenkins puffed, running into the room.

'Jenkins, I've been a complete fool and it's time to make things right. Fire up the jet packs—we need to get Ajay.'

'Very well, sir. Initiating jet pack take-off sequence right away.'

In no time at all they were flying high above London.

Joe spotted Ajay's house down below and signalled Jenkins to follow him.

A loud thump, a snapping of wood and several loud squeals later, Joe and Jenkins were hanging from the tree in Ajay's front garden.

'Are we down?' Jenkins asked, his eyes still tightly shut.

'Sort of . . .' Joe said, removing a woodpecker from his hair.

It just so happened that they were clinging to a branch opposite Ajay's bedroom window. He was sat at his desk, staring at Joe and Jenkins, open-mouthed.

'Ajay's mum is going to kill me,' Joe muttered.

'My mum is going to kill yooooooou!'

Ajay shouted, opening his window and leaning out. 'That's her apple tree you just ruined!'

Ajay was glaring at Joe, angrily.

'Look what you've done, you've ruined my tree!' Ajay's mum screamed as she came running out into the garden.

'Oh, Mrs Ajay, I'm so—'

'I always hated that thing! It's supposed to be an apple tree. I've only had one apple in twenty years. Thanks, Joe, you did me a favour. Now, can I get you boys anything? I've got a jalfrezi on the go—would you like some?'

'How about a ladder?' Jenkins asked, one eye open just a peek.

'Oh yes, of course. Where are my manners!'

Twenty minutes later they were all sitting in Ajay's front room. Joe and Jenkins were picking twigs and leaves out of their hair, while Ajay was perched on the edge of the sofa, looking at his feet.

Ajay's mum tutted loudly, breaking the awkward silence. 'Oh, this is ridiculous, you two! Don't you have anything to say to each other?'

Joe coughed to clear his throat. 'Ajay, I'm really, really sorry for saying all those things to you.'

'Mum,' Ajay started. 'You can tell Joe to stick his apology—'

'AJAY!' his mum snapped.

'That's all right, Mrs Ajay,' Joe said. 'I deserve it. I said some bad things to Ajay. Things that were hurtful.'

'And lies!' Ajay butted in.

'And lies,' Joe agreed. 'Truth is, I couldn't have been Prime Minister without you. I wouldn't want to be Prime Minister without you. I certainly can't fly a jet pack without you, and I wouldn't have taken part in the world's biggest high-five-a-thon, without you. I'm so sorry Ajay, and I need you back on my side.' Joe stood up and put his hand out for Ajay to shake.

'You got to be kidding me, right?' Ajay said. 'Shaking hands is for squares. I only high-five these days.' Ajay grinned and jumped up for a high-five. Joe jumped up to meet him, but misjudged it and high-fived Ajay's forehead instead.

It felt so good to have his best mate back.

There was a ring at the door.

'Joe? Your mum is here,' called Ajay's mum from the hallway. Before Joe could answer, his mum rushed in.

'I saw the jet pack and heard the crash so I figured you must be in town. Do I take it you two are friends now?'

Joe and Ajay nodded.

'Oh, thank goodness for that!'

'Mum, I saw you in that factory. When did you start working there?' Joe asked.

'Oh a few days ago now. I needed a job, and it's not as bad as all that . . .'

'Oh, Mum, I'm sorry—you belong in the park! I've really messed up but I'm sure I can fix it. You'll help me, won't you Ajay?'

Ajay nodded eagerly.

'Wait a sec,' said Joe, glancing at his watch. 'Why aren't you at school?'

'I got expelled.'

'What?!'

'Mr Brooks is well into this Anti-Silliness thing. No one is allowed to joke or smile anymore.

Although, since the Anti-Silliness League started up, he's never looked happier.' Ajay sighed. 'I hate to admit it Joe, but I'm . . . bored!'

'Right, I think it's time we did something about Violetta and her Anti-Silliness League. But first, we need to get back to Downing Street.'

While they were getting ready to leave, Jenkins' phone beeped with a message.

'Oooh . . .' said Jenkins, reading the screen. 'It seems that Violetta is organizing a vote of no confidence in you. Sir, she's making a play for the leadership.'

'She can't do that! I can explain to the people that I had a crisis of confidence but I'm OK now—people who love fun and people who hate it can live in harmony—we can find a way!'

'I'm afraid she's already done it. Sir, may I be frank?'

'Only if I can be Kevin.' Ajay laughed. 'Sorry, too soon . . . but man, it feels good to be back in the game!'

'Sir,' Jenkins persevered, ignoring Ajay, 'it pains me to say this, but I'm afraid there may be no way to beat her. Violetta is a shrewd political player and she's been one step ahead of us from the beginning. I've seen her type before—she's obsessed with power and there's nothing that she won't do to get her grubby hands on it. The park thing has given her a chance to get her claws in.'

'But everyone hates her!' Joe exclaimed. 'Why would they want her as Prime Minister?'

'A lot of people are scared of her, and, ultimately, will do as she tells them. Sir, if we'd had more time, perhaps we could have done something, but her Anti-Silliness League has grown too powerful.'

'What do you think I should do, Jenkins?'

'Sir . . . Joe . . . I think it's time for you to consider your position. I think you should tell her you're resigning and you're going to make her the next Prime Minister.'

Joe looked at Jenkins, his mum, and Ajay. The most important people in his life and the ones he had sworn not to let down. He had just decided to make things right and now he might never have the chance. Joe gulped.

'Jenkins, you've been the best advisor a Prime Minister could ever have and I trust you a hundred per cent. Can you set up a meeting with Violetta first thing tomorrow?'

'I think that's wise, Prime Minister. I'll let her know right away. And Ajay, I was wondering if you had your mobile computer and your wireless telephone here?'

'My laptop and phone you mean? Yes, why?'

'I wonder if we may spend some time working on . . . Joe's speech. Perhaps you could help?' Jenkins leaned in and whispered something to Ajay and Joe.

Joe and Ajay looked at each other and then nodded to Jenkins.

'OK, let's work on it together,' Joe said with steely determination.

IT AIN'T OVER
TILL IT'S OVER

The next morning, Joe slid down the fireman's pole, letting out the traditional squeal as he went. He was in a good mood, a really good mood for someone who was about to lose their job.

'Who's for a game of tag-team ker-plunk?' Joe called out to no one in particular.

'Sir?' Jenkins poked his head around the door of the cabinet room. 'What about Violetta . . .'

'Oh, I don't want to play ker-plunk with her!' Joe cringed.

'No, Prime Minister, Violetta's waiting . . .' Jenkins said, tapping his watch.

'Oh, of course! Yes, you're right, matters of national importance first, ker-plunk later.'

Joe walked down the hall to meet Violetta. Ajay caught Joe up on the way and fell into step by his side. Violetta was waiting next to the front door, with an evil look in her eye.

'Oh no, you're even more annoying than Perkins.' Violetta sneered at Ajay. 'Why are you here?'

'Just wanted to see it with my own eyes,' Ajay smiled calmly, staring at Violetta.

'If you'd like to come this way, Violetta,' said Joe, gesturing for her to follow him into the cabinet room.

Violetta took one look at the fireman's pole and jelly-eating facilities and shuddered. 'Ghastly. It'll all have to go.'

She turned to Joe and got a pen out of her jacket pocket. 'I hope you're not going to embarrass yourself by dragging this out? Just sign the papers and go home.'

'Jenkins, will you take Ajay to wait in the other room, please?' Joe asked.

'Of course, sir. If you need me, just call. You have your phone on you, don't you?'

Joe tapped his pocket. 'Yep.'

Joe led the way into the cabinet room, put his phone on the side and loosened his tie.

'Since when did you start wearing ties?' Violetta asked.

'Oh I don't really, it just goes with the suit.'

'That's your problem, Perkins, it's all just dressing up to you, isn't it? It's all about pretending and having fun.'

'What's wrong with fun?'

'Fun is pathetic and weak. Who needs fun when you can make money?' Violetta smirked. 'But what really gets to me the most, what really makes me sick, is the fact you are just a kid. Kids disgust me! Grotty little turnips with their sticky hands and runny noses. I hate their horrid faces and their stupid laughs. When I'm in charge we'll see if they feel like laughing after eighteen hours of school every day!'

'But you can't . . . !'

'I CAN DO WHAT I LIKE!' Violetta shouted triumphantly. Joe stood back while she started pacing the floor.

'And that's just the start. When the Anti-Silliness League comes to power, you can wave goodbye to play times, drawing, singing, books with happy endings. All gone! Eighteen hours of lessons a day, and into the workplace aged twelve. Every park in the land will be concreted over. Trees too, and beaches!

Everywhere that children find fun, I'll destroy and build more factories to make me rich. I'm not like you, Joe, I didn't come here with a vague plan of having fun and dressing up a bit. I'll do what I want and there's nothing you can do to stop me.' Violetta laughed loudly.

'But what about the Anti-Silliness League? You still need their support. I know they don't like me, but do they really want to see children being sent out to work?' Joe asked, scratching his head.

'They're just a snivelling bunch of busy-bodies! I own them!'

'I could tell the world what you're planning. What then?'

'Do you think they'd believe a grown-up or a child? One who can't even jump on a bouncy castle without it exploding? By the time I get into power it will be too late. I'll have the best team around me to ensure that I get exactly what I want.'

Joe leant against a bookcase, thoughtfully. 'Actually, I was thinking about that bouncy castle the other day. How did it pop exactly?'

'All it takes is a sharp pin, a good disguise, excellent timing, and KABOOOOOOM!'

'So it was you who sabotaged the re-opening of the park? Even the poo in the sandpit?!'

'I orchestrated the whole thing! And then I took a picture of you to sell to the papers. But good luck trying to prove it! Perhaps you can make another YouTube video about it, see how well that goes?'

'YouTube?' Joe laughed. 'Oh I've moved on from that. Do you know the great thing about mobile phones is they're not even really phones?' Joe picked his phone up from the side. 'I mean, take mine for instance. It's also a camera. You can even film stuff on it.'

'What?' Violetta hissed.

'You see this?' Joe said, pointing to the red flashing light at the bottom of his phone. 'Smile, you're on TV.'

Violetta's eyes grew wide and she tried to snatch the phone from Joe's hand. 'Give me that phone. I'm going to destroy it and then I'm going to destroy you!'

'Bit late for that I'm afraid. We fixed a live feed from

the phone to a laptop, which is being streamed to every news channel in the country. So much more impressive than making just another YouTube video, don't you agree?' Joe grinned. 'Guys, you can come in now.'

The doors opened and in walked Jenkins, Ajay, and Joe's mum.

'No, it can't be done!'

'Oh come now, Violetta, all you need is to set up a basic wi-fi signal that you can beam to every interface of every broadcaster in the country. It's a simple binary relay system using encrypted code sent through a wi-fi network,' said Ajay, smiling.

'Are you in on this, Jenkins?!' Violetta spluttered.

'Just because one wears a Windsor knot, doesn't mean one is too old to get a basic grasp of encrypted mobile technology. Isn't that right, Ajay?'

'You da man, Jenksy!'

'Why thank you, Master Patel. And you are indeed, my brother from another mother. Is that how one says it?'

'By now, Violetta, your speech should be all over the TV,' said Joe.

Jenkins grabbed a remote and turned the TV on. And there it was, the phone footage of Violetta's speech on every channel across the network.

'But . . . but I thought you were on my side, Jenkins!' Violetta shrieked.

'Yes, I was rather proud of my performance,' Jenkins replied, coolly. 'I used to act as a young lad at prep school. They still talk about my Bottom all these years later.'

Ajay fell on the floor laughing.

Jenkins sighed and rolled his eyes. 'Ajay, Bottom is a character in a play called *A Midsummer Night's Dream*, by William Shakespeare. Honestly, the youth of today . . .'

'We had a deal, Jenkins,' Violetta whimpered. 'I saw your Anti-Silliness badge . . .'

'I've spent a long time in politics, Violetta, and I've served many Prime Ministers—some good, some less so. I thought I was happy doing that until Joe came along. You see, he showed me that there are more important things in life than approval ratings and big business deals. Joe taught me that being kind, having empathy, and wanting people to enjoy themselves—these are the things we should all treasure. Being Prime Minister is about looking after your fellow countrymen and women, not forcing them to look after you.' Jenkins smiled. 'You don't belong in office, Violetta, you belong in jail.'

'Thank you, Jenkins,' said Joe, looking a little teary. 'Jenkins told me all about your little scheme. When he said I should resign, I was taken aback, until he told me the reason why. We had to make you believe you'd won. We had to wait for the right moment, wait until you thought I was backed into a corner and then all I had to do was press record and burst your bubble—KABOOOOM! There's a nice policeman outside who wants to talk to you about all this money you're planning on making from selling off the parks. As well as the criminal use of a fake dog poo. Still, prison won't be so bad—after all, I've just introduced a few new rules, like joke-telling classes and balloon-animal lessons. To teach people how much nicer it is to have fun, rather than commit nasty crimes like embezzlement and fraud!'

'You'll never take me alive!' yelled Violetta as she made a mad run for the open window. Jenkins gave a short whistle and a policeman came in, pulling Violetta back into the room and reading her her rights.

'Prime Minister?' Jenkins said. 'I think it's about time you faced your public.'

TO THE END

Joe strode out of Number Ten Downing Street, back towards the microphone that started this whole adventure. This time his head was held high. Plus, someone had remembered to leave a box for him to stand on.

'People of Britain. I've let you down when you needed me the most. I got scared and instead of facing my fears, I worried that I wasn't good enough and fell into a deep, jelly-related depression. I behaved badly to the people I care about the most and I'm sorry. All I ever wanted to do was make the world smile, but I realize that isn't possible all of the time. Perhaps I tried too hard to make everything fun, and maybe that's not always possible either. What I do know is that to live in a world with no fun, no laughter, and no joy—well that's no world at all.

Kids need time to enjoy being kids, but grown-ups need to be allowed to act like kids once in a while too. Opening the park again—properly this time—is just the beginning. If you will give me another chance, I promise not to let you down.'

'Tonight on Eye-Witness News with Charlie James: Joe Perkins' first year in charge, and what a year it's been! He's gone from a normal schoolboy, to the most famous child in the world, to Prime Minister, to the brink of losing it all. And yet here we are a year on and Joe is going strong. Tonight we remember what a year it's been. First up, I'd like to welcome a former member of the Anti-Silliness League.'

The camera switched to a darkened room, with a man sitting in shadow, concealing his identity. 'Tell me what happened to the Anti-Silliness League. Is it over?' Charlie asked.

'I'd say the movement's completely dead now. I mean, it started with good intentions. Some of us felt uncomfortable having so much fun, and then Violetta came along and I guess she seemed to tap into something. Well, we just went along with it, and before we knew what was happening we were chasing clowns out of town, picketing joke shops—you name it, we were doing it. Looking back now, it's all a bit embarrassing. I'm not sure what came over us. But when we saw Violetta for who she really was, well, things changed for all of us. The way she set Joe up, well, that's not on, is it?'

'And what are you doing now?' Charlie asked.

'I thought maybe if I joined in, I might actually have some fun. It started with dressing up at home, waiting for my wife to go out before slipping on a wig. Messing around with a big red nose and big shoes. And before I knew it, I was clowning around. That's when my wife caught me. I thought she'd be angry, but she's been really supportive. She persuaded me to give up my career as an accountant and now I've joined the circus.'

'Wow, that's quite a story. Thank you, sir.'

'Please, call me Chuckles.'

When the camera cut back to the studio, Charlie was sitting on a sofa with Violetta Crump.

'Violetta, welcome. Of course you've also had a busy year, heading up the Anti-Silliness League, followed by a short spell in prison. What's next for Violetta Crump?'

'So lovely to be here, Charlie. I'm so excited about the publication of my memoirs, *Enjoying Life*. It's all about my road to recovery and finding the real me. I just want to give something back. All profits go to the home for orphaned kittens, because for me it's not about making money, it's about being reborn into this new happy, fun-loving Violetta you see before you.' Violetta cocked her head to one side and smiled.

'You seemed to get out of prison awfully quickly—why was that?' Charlie asked.

'None of your business you nosy little . . . I mean, I have learnt my lesson, I was a model prisoner, I've served my time and now I'm ready to get back to being a productive member of society.' Violetta's smile widened.

'And what are your feelings about Joe Perkins?' Charlie asked.

'I'd like to thank Joe for teaching me a lesson. I can't wait to see him again to thank him personally,' she said through gritted teeth. 'If you're watching, Joe, I'm coming to get you. I mean, see you. Yep, I definitely meant "see you".'

'The Prime Minister's success continues,' said Charlie James, turning back to camera. 'In fact today he's off to celebrate his anniversary in the place where he spends almost every morning. The park.'

'So we're agreed, Mr President. Both our countries will do what we can to reduce the deficit?' asked Joe, smoothing down his hair.

'Absolutely, Prime Minister. I must say this is the first summit about fiscal policy,' the President said, unbuckling the seat belt, 'that I've ever conducted on a rollercoaster.'

'It's good, isn't it? What's more you get a photo as a memento from the booth at the end.' Joe handed the President the picture of them both upside down on the rollercoaster, and gave him a high-five before seeing him to his limo.

Joe loved the park in the morning. He wandered over to where his mum was trimming the flower beds.

'Looking good, Mum,' he said.

'Oh, thanks love. I'm really pleased. You've done a brilliant job with the fairground—and free for everyone too! I know when you suggested having a custard boating lake, I was sceptical. But what can I say? I was wrong, you were right.'

'Aw, thanks, Mum. Have you seen Ajay?' Joe asked.

'I think he's on the waltzers with Mr Brooks.'

Joe arrived at the waltzers just as Ajay was giving Mr Brooks a lecture.

'As education secretary and your boss, Mr Brooks, I do hope you'll be operating a "scream-if-you-want-to-go-faster" policy on this ride?'

'I keep trying to tell you, Ajay!' Mr Brooks yelled. 'I'm not a teacher anymore. I gave it all up to get away from the likes of you!'

'Wait a sec,' Ajay said, scratching his head. 'You gave up teaching and joined the fair to get away from kids?' Ajay looked around at the hundreds of children all over the park. 'Bad choice, Mr B, bad choice.'

'Hey, Ajay!' Joe yelled. 'The England captain's just arrived—do you fancy a kick-about?'

'Yeah, go on then, I was getting bored of annoying Mr Brooks anyway. See you same time tomorrow, Mr B!' Ajay yelled.

'Yes, Ajay, it's always such fun!' Mr Brooks sighed.

'Speaking of fun, where's the new Minister of Fun?' Joe said.

'Up here, sir!' Jenkins yelled. Ajay and Joe looked up to watch Jenkins do some impressive loop-the-loops with his jet pack.

'Nice skills!' Ajay yelled approvingly.

'I had a good teacher!' Jenkins bellowed.

'You're welcome!'

'Not you, Ajay, her!' Jenkins yelled, pointing further up into the sky.

None other than the Queen came thundering past on a jet pack. 'Who are you talking to, George?'

'Who's George?' Joe and Ajay said at the same time.

'I am!' Jenkins yelled.

'Never mind that!' the Queen called out.

'Pass me the catapult please, George!'

Jenkins passed her the royal catapult in mid-air.

'Why?'

'Because there's a pigeon on that bouncy castle!' she shouted.

Joe, Ajay and Jenkins all looked at each other.

'NOOOOOOOOOOOO!' they all shouted.

'Ready . . . aim . . . !' the Queen yelled.

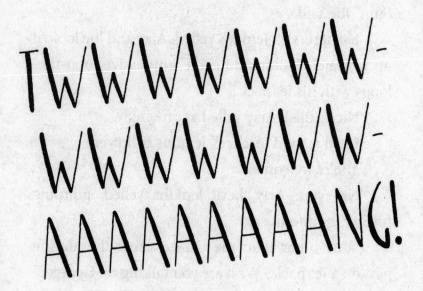

TWWWWWWW-WWWWWWW-AAAAAAAAANG!

ABOUT THE AUTHOR

Before becoming a writer and illustrator Tom spent nine years working as political cartoonist for *The Western Morning News* thinking up silly jokes about even sillier politicians. Then, in 2004 Tom took the plunge into illustrating and writing his own books. Since then he has written and illustrated picture books as well as working on animated TV shows for Disney and Cartoon Network. *The Accidental Prime Minister* is his debut children's novel.

Tom lives in Devon and his hobbies include drinking tea, looking out of the window, and biscuits. His hates include spiders and running out of tea and biscuits.

CONTINUE THE LAUGHS!

CHARLIE MERRICK'S MISFITS:
FOULS, FRIENDS & FOOTBALL

STINKBOMB & KETCHUP-FACE
AND THE BADNESS
OF BADGERS

OLIVER AND
THE SEAWIGS

THE DEMON
HEADMASTER

HERE BE MONSTERS!